GW01606113

DEATH UNDERGROUND

TERROR TRIOS

FEATURING WYATT BLASSINGAME

DEATH UNDERGROUND
TERROR TRIOS
FEATURING WYATT BLASSINGAME

INTRODUCTION BY

JOHN PELAN

BOSTON
ALTUS PRESS
2012

© 2012 Altus Press • First Edition—2012

EDITED AND DESIGNED BY

Matthew Moring

PUBLISHING HISTORY

"Floridian Fiends" appears here for the first time. Copyright © 2012 John Pelan. All Rights Reserved.

"Ghouls of the Green Death" originally appeared in the June, 1934 issue of *Dime Mystery Magazine*. Copyright © 1934 by Popular Publications, Inc. Copyright renewed © 1961 and assigned to Argosy Communications, Inc. All Rights Reserved.

"We Danced With Death!" originally appeared in the August, 1936 issue of *Terror Tales*. Copyright © 1936 by Popular Publications, Inc. Copyright renewed © 1963 and assigned to Argosy Communications, Inc. All Rights Reserved.

"Death Underground" originally appeared in the January, 1934 issue of *Dime Mystery Magazine*. Copyright © 2012 Argosy Communications, Inc. All Rights Reserved. Reprinted by arrangement with Argosy Communications, Inc.

Published by arrangement with Argosy Communications, Inc.

THANKS TO

Joel Frieman, Rick Ollerman, John Pelan & David White

ALL RIGHTS RESERVED

No part of this book may be reproduced or utilized in any form or by any means, electronic or mechanical, without permission in writing from the publisher.

This edition has been marked via subtle changes, so anyone who reprints from this collection is committing a violation of copyright.

Visit altuspress.com for more books like this.

Printed in the United States of America.

TABLE OF CONTENTS

WYATT BLASSINGAME

FLORIDIAN FIENDS

WITH THIS, the second volume of "Terror Trios" we are proud to present three stellar examples of the work of the author we feel is the finest practitioner in the weird tales field that no one seems to be familiar with. Considering the prodigious quantity and remarkably high quality of his work during the 1930s one would expect Wyatt Blassingame to be mentioned in the same breath as contemporaries such as Lovecraft, Smith, and Howard. Certainly, he was as important to the success of Popular Publications' "Big Three" weird menace pulps as the aforementioned gentlemen were to the success of *Weird Tales.*

Between 1934 and 1940 Wyatt Blassingame authored over five dozen outstanding horror stories; almost all were for Popular Publications and the vast majority were of at least novelette length and frequently they had the place of honor as the cover story. Such a track record should have served to make the author a well-known figure within the genre. Sadly, this was not to be the case.... The reasons for Blassingame's obscurity are ironically enough a result of his success!

First and foremost, with the exception of a handful of reprint anthologies edited and published by Robert Weinberg over twenty years ago and two fine anthologies edited by the late Sheldon Jaffrey, the weird menace pulps have been pretty much ignored by anthologists, with only a handful of tales by Hugh B. Cave appearing in the massive collections of his pulp fiction published by Fedogan & Bremer. Until recently, with the advent of "Terror Trios" here at Altus Press and a five-volume set of Blassingame's collected weird tales in process at Dancing Tuatara Press, only one volume (a slim paperback collection of detective stories which was published over fifty years ago) existed as evidence of Wyatt Blassingame's career as a pulpster.

The main reason for the weird menace pulps being ignored is a partially deserved reputation for formulaic tales of cardboard characters with the main emphasis being on wild excesses of violence and hints of all manner of depravity. While true to a certain extent, a sweeping generalization like this is no more accurate or useful than to state that *Weird Tales* published the worst science fiction of the 1930s. Again, a true statement, but one that ignores all of the fine work published there.

The truisms are that editor Rogers Terrill was fond of the formula where a seemingly supernatural menace would be revealed to be of a mundane nature on the last page of the story. Equally true is that when the genre was bad, it was awful.... However, the mainstays of the "Big Three" *(Dime Mystery Magazine, Horror Stories,* and *Terror Tales)* such as Blassingame, Knox, Ernst, Cave, Zagat, & Burks were talented enough to get the most out of the formula and more importantly, were popular enough that they could blithely ignore the editorial mandate and turn in out-and-out supernatural tales whenever they chose to do so. The results were a body of work that can stand comparison to the best stories in *Weird Tales* or *Strange Tales.* In the case of Wyatt Blassingame, he started at a high level in 1934 and remained in top form until the genre imploded in the late 1930s.

To add a bit more background, I'd like to address the canard that has floated around collecting circles for many years; the idea that somehow the aforementioned authors weren't good enough to crack *Weird Tales*.... Obviously, Burks, Cave, and Ernst were so prolific that they were frequent contributors to "The Unique Magazine" as all three men were capable of filling a magazine's complete content. In the cases of Blassingame and Knox there's a very pragmatic reason why they ignored *Weird Tales*... they were earning two to three times as much appearing in the "Big Three!" One might also take note of the fact that during the height of the weird menace genre (1935-1937) both Arthurs (Burks and

Zagat) are pretty much absent from *Weird Tales,* presumably with only overflow tales being submitted there.

While Wyatt Blassingame did write a wide variety of fiction, it's evident that with his knowledge of obscure mythologies and cultures that the genre of weird fiction was perfectly suited to his talents. Of the three novellas presented here, two are from his first year as a professional writer and serve to show just how polished his work was from the very beginning. Throughout the 1930s he remained one of, if not the best of the authors specializing in the genre. Equally comfortable with Terrill's formula or with the full-blown supernatural tale, his stories provide a great mix and keep the reader guessing as to whether or not the horror is supernatural or not. As the decade wound to a close and the weird menace genre perished due to its self-imposed limitations Blassingame switch to more straightforward detective and mystery tales and proved to be equally good at those.

Called into service in WWII, Blassingame returned to find a vastly different market from what he had left.... The weird menace genre was gone entirely with only an occasional story of that type showing up here and there. The pulps themselves were dying, where once over two dozen mystery and horror pulps dominated the newsstands now there were only a handful of digest-sized magazines in their stead. Wyatt Blassingame saw the handwriting on the wall and immediately made the switch to authoring children's books on a variety of subjects (most often U.S. History). Later he would augment his income by teaching creative writing.

Apparently, these new careers left little time to contemplate marketing collections of his pulp fiction and thus, some of the finest weird fiction of the 1930s has remained unavailable.... Until now.... If you enjoy these three novellas, we suggest checking out the first two volumes of Wyatt Blassingame's selected weird tales, *The Tongueless Horror* and *Lady of the Yellow Death;* both available from Dancing Tuatara Press at www.ramblehouse.com.

John Pelan
Midnight House
Gallup, NM

WYATT BLASSINGAME

GHOULS OF THE GREEN DEATH

Like some dread nightmare beast, the Green Death stalked the streets of New York, invading the homes of the innocent, leaving men in hideous agony from which there was no escape. And Detective Fred Kane, seeking the fiend behind this holocaust, found even himself a victim of the hideous pestilence—his body a living fire of pain, his brain a tortured Thing that saw death creeping inevitably upon it!

FRED KANE looked out at the rolling darkness of the huge cemetery and a shudder ran through his tall, angular body. For just one second fear was a wet coldness along his spine. Then he laughed and wondered why he had shuddered. The cemetery was peaceful enough. A three-quarter moon hung low in the west, making the grass look ebony and silver. White tombstones were pale death flowers blooming in the moonlight. Far down the gravel drive he could see the dark blot of the caretaker's cottage. Peaceful—yet Kane had shuddered in sudden fear looking across the moon-washed slopes.

Twenty-four hours later he was to remember that shudder and experience the weird feeling of predestined evil that may come to a man who watches something that he has dreamed actually happen.

But now Kane shrugged. "Maybe I better give up my job with the force and start selling lavender perfume—me getting the jitters from looking at a marble orchard!"

He turned, crossed the street, and walked north half a block to the subway station. His shoes made thudding sounds on the concrete steps as he went down.

The clock over the change booth said 2:32. Kane yawned, dropped a nickel in the turnstile and pushed through. Damn, he was tired. Ten hours he'd been tampling about upper Manhattan and hadn't learned a thing which would help a cop who was a member of the Missing Persons Bureau to find four guys who'd disappeared recently. This was no job for a detective who liked his troubles breaking fast and with something new on the ball each time. It had sounded interesting, however.

Four persons had disappeared within the last week, all from the same section—and all of them young and healthy. A girl had gone to put some flowers on her Aunt Emma's grave, and never came back. Two young men had started downtown late at night—they must have ridden this subway, Kane thought—and nothing had been heard of them since. One man had left his downtown office late, headed to his home on West 158th Street. He'd never gotten there....

Kane looked up and down the bleakly lighted platform. The only other person waiting was a small, bow-legged man in a brown suit near the far end. He stood with his back turned to Kane. Trains didn't run often at this time of the night. The detective dug in his hip pocket, pulled out a newspaper.

GREEN DEATH STRIKES DOWN TWO MORE, the streamer howled. Kane wrinkled the mouth that looked surprisingly young and boyish in his dark, angular face, and made a snorting noise. That was the trouble with these papers trying to build up circulation, he thought—always playing up scare stories. He'd read the previous stories about the Green Death and he started reading this one without much interest.

Abruptly, then, his fingers tightened about the paper and his black head bent closer.

FIVE more persons had contracted the disease which scientists had as yet been unable to identify. The child of one of New York's most prominent millionaires entered the hospital last week with the disease, had died. His face had been a vivid, horrible green before his death and his last hours had been in agony which morphine could not relieve. Doctors were fearful that an epidemic might spread through the city. Scientists admitted they were without means to fight the plague should it gain further headway.

One of the two new patients was a young man of moderate means, average family. Another was an old pauper from the Bowery. No man could know at what moment the plague might strike him. The millionaire had offered a large reward for his son's cure, and was allowing the offer to stand after the boy's death—as an incentive to medical effort which might save others from a similar fate. But so far all the furious efforts of science had been futile. Horrible agony and sure death awaited the person who contracted the disease.

Fred Kane's long, hard fingers knotted as they gripped the paper. Death from knives and guns he didn't fear. He'd looked at Death often, and grinned in his face. But this sort of thing—it didn't give a man a chance.

Kane shrugged and looked up the track for the train. Not in sight yet.

Abruptly the detective's tall, lean body stiffened. His eyes squinted almost shut. "What the hell?" he said aloud.

The bow-legged man in the brown suit had vanished. He couldn't have left the platform without coming back past Kane. He hadn't done that, yet he was gone!

The newspaper slid rustling from Kane's hand. He began to walk with long, swinging strides toward the point where the man had stood. His right shoulder was slightly higher than his left, making a hollow between his coat and shirt on the left side. Through that hollow his right hand could reach and pull a .38 police special in less than one second.

Fred Kane was a tall man. His shoulers looked too wide above his long, straight legs and hipless waist. His face was dark, with high, prominent cheekbones and a lean, hard chin. His nose was straight, high-bridged. His forehead was high, his hair straight and black. He was thirty years old, looked forty until one noticed his mouth and eyes. Then you thought he might be no more than twenty. The mouth was wide, pleasant. The eyes were surprisingly light brown in his dark face. As a rule they held a boyish twinkle. Now they had suddenly gone dead and colorless.

Kane reached the point where the bow-legged man had stood, looked around. No doors here. He stepped to the edge of the platform, looked over. The squinted eyes followed the steel tracks out into the dimly lighted tunnel.

Kane's mouth jerked wide open and his eyes seemed abruptly to swell. His cheek bones made sharp creases across his face. "God!" he said.

Along the tunnel occasional dust-coated globes threw dim patches of light. The dark figures looked like weird, abnormal shadows. For one second Kane stood motionless, amazed, staring.

There were three of them. Tall, black, flowing things that seemed to glide along the floor of the tunnel. And over the top of one, hanging as limp as an empty bag, was the bow-legged man in the brown suit. Kane could see his arm swaying slightly as the thing below him glided.

"Hey!" The word was a bellow that shook along the concrete tunnel. Kane flung his long body from the edge of the platform, hit between the tracks running. The .38 special was gripped hard in his right hand.

The tall, gliding things stopped, turned. They were nearly a hundred yards away, but Kane was eating up the distance with amazing speed.

Abruptly they twisted away from Kane, and leaped.

The dusky light from a shaded bulb shone on them for a second before they whipped into the gloom beyond. The cold lump went out of Kane's chest and his lips turned up in a hard grin. Those things were men in long, black robes.

"Hey!" he yelled, kept running. "Stop or I'm shootin'!"

THE last words were drowned out by a low but growing thunder. The train was coming.

The figures were less than sixty yards ahead now. Kane's right hand began to steady in front of him, centering the gun. The thunder had grown to a roar and he could see the light of the train beyond the running men. It was coming toward him at fifty miles an hour,

Without warning the three men stopped. They were at the edge of a circle of light and Kane could see the swaying robes, the black, pointed hoods, the dangling arms of the bow-legged man. They were to the left of the tracks, but the light of the train caught them for a second. As it did one raised a slow hand, threw back the hood from about his face. Kane caught a sharp, terrified breath. The face below the hood was a livid green!

The train was even with them now, past them, and howling toward Kane. He heard the wild screaming of brakes. He leaped to the left and his foot hit a cross tie, sent him spinning. He tried to catch his balance, staggered and went crashing down straight toward the third rail.

Wild terror lashed at him. He'd seen men die in the chair, eyes bulging from their heads. The third rail held the same death. He tried to fling his body back from the rail, across the tracks in front of the oncoming train. The brakes were screaming like a mad banshee now, making the long tunnel horrid with sound. Kane caught a glimpse of the first car thirty yards away, tearing at him.

He struck on his right side, right arm outflung. His hand rapped the protective plank above the rail. His ribs were across the track. The train was twenty yards away and coming fast.

Kane's legs doubled like pistons under him, straightened. His body plunged through space. He cleared the rail, shot between the upright pillars, hit between the next pair of tracks. The train howled over the spot where he had fallen, came to a jerking, shrieking halt.

Kane got unsteadily to his feet. He felt a little sick at his stomach and his knees were weak. He looked with wide eyes at the wheels which had almost ground him into a pulp, the high-powered third rail which he had missed by inches.

The engineer had craned his neck around the front of the train and was yelling back at Kane. "What the God damned holy hell do you—" White, frightened faces were peering from the train windows.

Abruptly Kane broke into a furious race toward the rear of the train. Behind him the engineer kept up his shouting. Kane, too, cursed as he ran. Those hooded men would be getting away while he stood here like a ninny.

He sprinted past the last car, leaped the third rail, over the tracks and jerked to a halt near the concrete wall. Close around here. His eyes glinted up and down the tracks.

The hooded men and their captive had vanished.

CHAPTER TWO

The Missing Return

FOR TEN seconds Fred Kane stood flat-footed, staring along the dimly lighted tunnel. His eyes, which had been wide with surprise, narrowed slowly and the color went out of them. The high cheekbones began to show plainly across his face. Those hooded men couldn't have vanished into air—even if the face of one was a ghastly green. A cold shudder ran down Kane's back as he thought of that face.

Persons were calling from the train window now and Kane turned, saw two men start along the side of the cars toward him. The engineer and a conductor. Kane's full boyish mouth pressed into a straight line. It was just possible that the hooded men had—

"Hey! What the hell you think this is? A race track? Of all the damned fools...." The engineer was sputtering profanity as he approached.

Kane said, "Aw shut up." He flicked the lapel of his gray suit, showed the badge. "I was chasing a bunch of guys through here, but they got away. How far to the first emergency exit?"

The conductor pointed a stubby finger. "Hundred yards or more, maybe two hundred."

Kane nodded and the line of his mouth straightened. It was hardly conceivable that the men could have reached the emergency exit in those few seconds. If they hadn't escaped that way there was only one other place they could be—on the train.

Leaving the conductor at the rear to keep a lookout, Kane went with the engineer to the front, boarded the train and went through it. He didn't expect to find any hooded men; they would have removed those. But he found no discarded robes, no bow-legged man in a brown suit. None of the passengers had noticed anyone enter the train.

Finally Kane gave up the search. It didn't seem possible the men could have reached the emergency exit—yet they had vanished. He shrugged, told himself they were fast runners. But doubt and a strange, unaccountable fear gnawed at Kane's mind. There had been something supernatural, something eerie and horrible about those green-faced ghouls who had snatched the man from the subway platform and disappeared into the depths of this grimy, concrete tunnel.

Was this the way the other four had disappeared? Who were these robed, skulking figures who hid their rotting faces under dark hoods? Why were they stealing human beings and where did they vanish with them? "They must have reached that exit," Kane said, half aloud. But the very words seemed to mock him.

He called the conductor aboard, and the train pulled into the station where Kane had stood fifteen minutes earlier.

He left the cars and pushed through the turnstile. The clock above the change booth said 2:56. Inside the booth a man was nodding sleepily.

Kane stepped to the booth, peered through the glass. The man inside looked up with a start, pushed a couple of nickels toward the window. He was a short, plump, middle-aged man. His face was as round as a full moon, bald across the forehead and with a fringe of gray hair in the back. His skin was pink, his small mouth surprisingly white. His faded blue eyes were narrow and crafty.

Kane showed his badge, asked, "Anybody leave this station in the last few minutes?"

The man shook his round head. A pale light showed in the faded eyes. "How come?"

Kane said shortly, "Your damn certain nobody left here, or have you been asleep?"

A pale tongue showed between the man's white lips, vanished. "Nobody left this side. Maybe on the uptown side. I don't notice over there."

Kane said, "Okay." For a moment he looked at the round-faced man out of narrowed, colorless eyes. Heeling about, he walked out of the station.

IT was five minutes of ten when Fred Kane came down the walk toward the big brick building on Centre Street. He was carrying a newspaper in his hand and his boyish mouth was a bit stiff and pale.

Two men in uniform were on the steps as Kane started up them. They were big men, but there was something strained and frightened about their faces. Unconsciously they edged away from Kane and from each other.

The detective stopped. There was a question in his brown eyes, but his mouth was smiling. "What the hell, man? You think I got dandruff?"

The policeman shifted from one foot to the other. He asked grimly, "You seen the morning papers?"

Kane said, "Yes." The Green Death had been smeared all through them. Ten new cases in the city. On the subway this morning Kane had noticed many pale, frightened faces, eyes that nervously studied the other riders. There hadn't been the usual crowding.

The policeman blurted, "Well, the papers ain't got nothing about Ed Hammond beginning to yell with a headache right in here—less'n a hour ago." The man stopped, but his lips kept twitching.

Kane said, "God!" He felt hollow inside as he went on up the steps.

Inspector McFarlane listened to his story, wriggled his square jaw, and asked, "You're sure the man's face was green?"

Kane said, "Yes, sir. A sort of nasty looking green."

"That sort of ties up with a report we got in this morning," McFarlane said. "One of the men you were searching for, Ed Nabors, 326 West 158th Street, was found this morning." The inspector paused, wriggled his square jaw. Then he added: "A Dr. Peter McGrath was arrested when this fellow was seen in his car, throwing a fit. McGrath's from the Medical Center. He claimed he saw this fellow tossing a fit on the sidewalk, picked him up and started for the hospital with him. The reason he was throwing the fit—" McGrath paused again—"he had this Green Death."

Kane sucked a deep breath, felt the prickling of fear along his back. He was thinking of men dying in agony, not even able to fight against the thing that killed them. If a man was killed in a fight, that was one thing. But to be murdered by a little germ that crawled through your body, that you couldn't even see, couldn't put your hands on and fight....

The inspector said, "I can't be certain, but it looks as though there might be a definite tie-up between this disease and the missing persons. The police will have to do their part. The whole city, even the force, is getting jumpy."

Kane nodded. If the tie-up between the Green Death and the increasing number of missing persons was discovered, the city would become panic-stricken.

The inspector's square jaw set. He snapped, "I want some action."

Kane said, "Yes, sir." He turned on his heels. "I'll go out to the Medical Center and check on Nabors."

DR. PETER McGRATH was a slim, blond man with a button nose and rimless glasses. With him now was Dr. Charles Stuart, average height, lean, with a bald forehead, eyes and nose like a hawk.

"I suppose you want to see me about the Nabors man," McGrath said. His voice was slow and drawling, almost insulting. His blue eyes were hostile behind the glasses.

"You're right," Fred Kane answered. "I want you to tell me what you can about this disease, and about finding the young man."

McGrath licked his thin lips. "Dr. Stuart knows more about the disease than I. That's why he came down with me."

Kane looked toward the lean, hawk-faced doctor. Stuart said, "There's really very little I can tell you." He spoke rapidly, clipping the ends of the words. "We don't know how long after the time of contraction before the first symptoms appear. The first indication of which we know is a raging, intermittent headache, accompanied by high temperature. This generally lasts for one day. By the second day the patient's face begins to take on the greenish color, and by the end of that day he has generally gone mad from pain if not from some actual effect of the disease on the brain. Due to occasional hallucinations, I am inclined to believe the disease does affect the brain. The patients may linger for several days or may die as early as the third day."

Once more Fred Kane felt the chill breath of unknown fear against his face. His voice was husky as he said, "Ed Nabors disappeared four days ago. That means that he caught the disease *after* he disappeared."

"Not necessarily," Stuart clipped. "But to the best of our present knowledge, yes."

Kane ran a tongue over lips that were straight and hard. "May I see him?"

Flame jumped in Stuart's hawk eyes, went out. Dr. McGrath drawled, "You realize that we don't know how this disease is contracted. There is a possibility that by entering the patient's room...."

Kane swallowed at the lump in his throat. If he had been entering a room to shoot it out with a gangster, he would have gone smiling. But this—this was different. He swallowed again, said, "I'm working on this case. It would be best if I saw—the thing."

"You're the law," Stuart said sharply.

The girl bit her lips to keep them steady. Kane leaned suddenly forward, asked, "Are you Miss Nabors?"

She nodded.

Kane said, "I was at your home yesterday but couldn't find you." He introduced himself.

"The girl's in no condition to talk to detectives," McGrath drawled.

Kane swung half about to face the doctor. Rose Nabors put her hand on his arm.

"If there's anything I can tell that might help," she said, "I'll be glad to."

Kane said, "Thanks. Your brother wasn't having headaches before he left home, was he?"

Her blue eyes widened. "No. He'd always been so healthy, went in for athletics."

"Did he have any enemies? Anybody that might have wanted to hurt him, get him out of the way?"

She shook her head slowly. "Everybody liked Ed. He was always laughing and—" Her voice broke and a white line of perfect teeth showed as she bit her lower lip.

Abruptly Kane wanted to put his arms around her. Involuntarily he raised his hands. He stopped them, staring at his upturned palms. He had just come from the room of the Green Death. Suppose he had brought the disease with him. If he touched her....

"Thanks," he said, and turned abruptly away.

But when he left the hospital a few minutes later, the vision of tawny hair above a face had once again eclipsed the memory of that other, more horrible face.

THE cemetery fascinated Kane. Looking at it again now in the moonlight he could feel once more that strange shudder along his spine. He cursed himself for a fool, looked at his watch. Three minutes to twelve. He started back toward the subway entrance.

He'd come back to this section at twilight, had been walking nervously about since then. Five persons had disappeared in this neighborhood. Perhaps there would be others.

He went down the steps into the subway, stopped at the change booth. The pink-faced, bald-headed man glared at him out of furtive blue eyes. "Naw, I seen no bow-legged man in a brown hat. And nobody come out of this subway that didn't come in it on a train."

"All right," Kane said. "Keep your shirt on." He went over the turnstile without dropping a nickel, walked from end to end of the platform. Along the tunnel the dust-coated lights burned dully, the concrete wall showed in checkered light and shadow fading into dim nothingness. There was no life, no movement. He went back over the turnstile. From behind the glass door the bald-headed man watched him narrowly.

On the sidewalk again, Kane could see the cemetery, silver and black in the moonlight. There was a thick, six-foot hedge between it and the sidewalk, but from the opposite side of the street he could see over without trouble. He turned north, walking slowly.

A half block away a street light made a white circle on the pavement, one edge reaching up to the walk. Kane saw a man come into the light, then out again, moving with long swinging strides. For no reason he could name, Kane stood still and watched. He could scarcely see the man against the dark shadow of the hedge.

The man reached the drive which led in to the cemetery. There was no hedge here and for one half-second he showed clear and black against the moonlight.

And then, without warning, three hooded figures showed suddenly beside the man! Like giant and hideous geni they seemed to have risen out of the earth. Kane saw the man spin, heard the terrified cry that split his lips—and was cut short. A robed arm swung high and down. The black figures scooped up the man and vanished behind the hedge....

CHAPTER THREE

OUT OF THE GRAVE

IT HAD happened in less than two seconds, but before the figures disappeared, Fred Kane was running full tilt toward them, a .38 police special in his right hand. Hard muscles drove his legs like pistons; his shoulders were pushed forward; his breath came through clenched teeth from which the lips had curled back.

And deep in his belly cold fear gnawed at his bowels.

He wasn't afraid of three to one against him, but in his mind was that horrible green face he had seen below a back-thrown hood—and the agonized, pain-wracked face in the hospital!

His shoes pounded across the street, skidded on the gravel drive. He hit the soft green turf to the right of the drive, running at full blast—and stopped. The hooded figures had vanished!

The hair along Kane's neck was stiff and tingling. Nothing but a bird could have escaped in the few seconds that had elapsed. His eyes ached as he stared out into the moonlight, and that cold, shuddery fear quivered along his back. Last night they had vanished from the subway. And now....

Kane started walking, following the hedge. His eyes were narrowed to slits, and colorless. His mouth was straight and pale. He tried to shake off the fear that gripped him. Those men couldn't be suffering from the Green Death. If so, they'd be throwing fits, not kidnaping young men and women. Yet—their faces were green. A man had disappeared, and returned with the Green Death.

Kane cursed himself for a cowardly fool, swung out toward the center of the cemetery. They had to be here somewhere. Behind a tombstone perhaps.

Monuments of all sizes and shapes rose like weird stalagmites out of the ground around him. Ahead was the dark blot of a large mausoleum. To either side of it small oak trees showed like floating shadows in the moonlight.

Something flickered from the mausoleum to the oak—and vanished! Fred Kane caught one harsh breath and hurled himself forward, running in a zigzag line, gun ready.

A tongue of fire licked the darkness. A shot crashed. Wind whipped Kane's face and he heard the hiss of a bullet past his ear. He hurled himself to the right, hit flat on his chest, rolled back of a grave.

He slipped his gun across the top of the slab. He pushed one eye past the corner, peered at the spot from which the shot had come. The tree trunk was slender and dark. It bulged slightly on one side.

Kane centered the muzzle of his gun on the bulge, and shouted, "This is the police. Come from back of that tree or I'm shooting!"

The bulge in the tree quivered slightly. A voice asked, "Well, why in hell ain't yuh said so?" Then a dark shadow detached itself from the tree and moved forward. Kane could see the rifle in the man's hand.

"Drop that rifle," he said. "Then come ahead."

The man bent, lowered the rifle tenderly, straightened. Three steps and he was in the moonlight. Kane got up, pistol ready, and went to meet him.

It was an old man with stooped shoulders and shaggy white hair that fell across a narrow forehead. Eyes that were too close together were strangely bright in the wrinkled face. The mouth was toothless and the lips caved in over the gums. Somewhere Fred Kane had seen that face before.

KANE'S gun was close against his hip. He asked, "Who in hell are you?"

"I oughta be askin' you that question."

The man's voice was surprisingly deep with an unmistakable Bowery accent. "You come bustin' inta my cemetery. I'm the caretaker."

Kane nodded, kept trying to remember where he had seen the old man before. "Why the devil were you shooting at me?"

"There's been bad things goin' on in this place the last week. A woman yellin' four, five nights ago. Tonight I heard a man shout. Then I seen you come runnin' with that gun. Yuh want me to wait till yuh stuck it in my ribs and pulled the trigger?"

Kane's eyes were thin lines in his face now. He asked suddenly, "What's your name?"

The old man's white head jerked erect. The eyes blazed, then clouded like those of a hawk. "Ike Neganzi."

Breath made a hissing sound between Kane's teeth. Now he remembered! Ike Neganzi had been a small-time political racketeer. He'd been convicted, sentenced to thirty years and had gone up swearing to have revenge on the city which had imprisoned him. Two years ago he had been released, still swearing revenge. The city had offered him the job of caretaker at the cemetery and he had accepted. The papers had played it up for a day or two with pictures.

Could this man still hate the city so much that...?

Kane shrugged, stuck his gun back in its holster. "You see anybody else before you saw me? Men with hoods?"

Stark terror showed in the old man's face. "Not tonight. No!"

Kane tensed, leaning forward; lips pulled thin. "What do you mean, 'Not tonight'?"

"I seen them other nights." The sunken lips shook. "They got—green faces!"

For a half minute Kane stood motionless while dread ate slowly through his stomach. Before his slitted eyes was a vision of the face he had seen in the hospital: green and rotting, twitching with constant, unrelievable agony. Now, it was his job to run down these green-faced monsters. And if he succeeded and ran them to earth, it might mean—the Green Death for him.

Ike Neganzi said, "I'm gettin' on back to my house. I don't like it out here with—with...." His voice trailed off. He turned, picked up his rifle and started back toward the caretaker's lodge.

Kane went toward the point where the hooded men and their victim had vanished behind the hedge. From there he began a slow, systematic search. There *had* to be some sign to show where they had gone. They couldn't vanish as if they had changed into tombs—*as if they were ghouls which had risen from the grave and returned to the grave!*

Kane stopped his search, stood flat-footed, cursing himself. If he let his mind run on like this he'd go nuts. The way he had shuddered last night when looking at this cemetery. No reason for that. And now....

The sound that broke off all thought was sharp, flesh-crawling, like the grate of stone on stone. It snapped Fred Kane's muscles like a bolt of electricity, whirled him about, hand jumping for his gun.

The hand froze in sheer horror. Fear jerked his muscles into cold knots knocked the air from his lungs. His eyes began to swell in their sockets, unbelieving.

Moonlight lay bleak across the thick turf, the white tombs. And out of a grave beside Kane a Thing was rising! His distended eyes saw it for only one rushing second. It came straight up like a rising pillar of black smoke. Below it he could see the dark, emptiness of the grave. It cracked forward and down.

Kane tried to hurl himself to one side, to whip his hand beneath his coat and reach the .38. Fear-cold muscles moved sluggishly. They seemed to creak and strain with infinite slowness.

The Thing smashed into his head. Moonlight- burst into whirling pieces, faded into blackness.

A PATIENT, unending river of night flowed over and through Fred Kane. He could feel his body floating in it, merged into it so that darkness flowed around him like air and through him like blood.

There was something else in the black river, something hard and fragmentary. Parts of it touched on raw, pained nerves.

The river of darkness faded into light but the tiny fragments became harsher, more numerous. Kane stirred, tried subconsciously to avoid them and could not. His eyes were open, but it was a long minute before they began to focus and his brain functioned.

With the suddenness of a bell ceasing to ring, one thought beat furiously in Kane's brain. He was afraid, horribly, unreasoningly afraid! He tried to hurl himself into terrified movement, felt his muscles jerk and become still.

Then sight returned to his eyes and thought to his mind.

He was lying flat on his back, his hands tied behind him, his feet bound together. High above him was a curving roof of solid concrete. His eyes followed this down to where it met the dirt floor on which he lay. He twisted his head, looked toward the other side. Here too was a solid concrete wall. Fastened to it, about shoulder high, was a gasoline lamp that made white, glaring light. About ten yards below his feet a black curtain formed one wall and another made the fourth behind his head. It occurred to him suddenly that he must be in an abandoned subway tunnel.

These things Kane saw and recognized though his entire being was concentrated on the thing which had flung cold fear through his body. He knew now what the jarring fragments in the river of darkness had been.

From beyond the curtain at his feet came a steady torrent of noise. Fred Kane had never heard those sounds before, but he recognized them. They were incessant, short, high-pitched—but flat and wailing.

Beyond that curtain someone was suffering the horrors of hell, someone had gone mad with pain—and was screaming.

Like furious, pointed barbs of agony the sounds came, one on top of the other, unending. They jangled at Kane's nerves, curdled his brain into a quivering, pulsating horror.

Kane's mouth jerked open to cry out against the torture of the sounds. Then his jaw clamped tight. He began to wriggle against his bonds, writhing, twisting. The ropes held, but when he stopped to rest he had moved several yards toward the green curtain.

Kane's jaw was knotty with muscle and his cheekbones showed pink. He began to roll toward the curtain. From beyond it the screams came, high and flat.

Lying close against the curtain, Kane caught the bottom of it with his teeth, rolled his head. For just one second he stared through the space below the curtain—yet that second remained indelibly stamped on his brain. That second dragged itself throughout aeons of time while Kane ached to shut his eyes against the sight at which he gazed, frozen in horror, unable to move. Then he was rolling back across the floor, vomiting.

Just beyond the curtain had been iron bars which reached from side to side of the tunnel. Beyond the bars was a room similar to his own, lighted in the same way. The man from whom the screams had come lay in the middle of the dirt floor.

HE was undressed except for underwear. The flesh of his body was a sickening, rotting green. His hands and feet were tied, but he twitched ceaselessly against the ropes, flopping about in an agony that lashed utterly exhausted muscles into movement. His eyes had been toward Kane, green, mad eyes. His mouth was open and saliva drooled nastily across his chin and throat. Constant twitching had rubbed the skin from his shoulders and legs, making great, dirt crusted, bloody sores. From his open mouth the cries tore like the wild screaming of a ripsaw.

For two minutes Fred Kane lay weak and sick. His brain was whirling and fear crowded his lungs against the walls of his chest. The man beyond the curtain was dying of the Green Death. Why had he been brought here to die? Why had Kane been brought to this subterranean vault? Did it mean that he too…? God!

He began to fight like a madman against the ropes that held him. The skin cracked and started to ooze blood, but the bonds held.

Abruptly Kane quit struggling. He lay very still, head half raised from the floor, listening. Below the constant, jarring screams there had been another sound.

It came again, nearer. A muffled voice speaking, the pad of shoes. An iron hinge grated and Kane knew that someone had entered the room of the dying man.

Rolling as silently as possible. Kane reached the curtain again, lifted it with his teeth. Blood drained from his dark face, leaving it a sickly yellow, as he watched.

Three men had entered the death room. They wore surgeon's white clothes and surgeon's masks. Rubber gloves covered their hands. As Kane watched two of them knelt beside the bound man. One held a hypodermic. The other caught the green man's shoulder, pushed him over on one side. The thin needle of the hypo plunged into the green flesh on the inside of the elbow. As the gloved hand pulled back on the plunger, the bowl of the hypodermic was filled with blood.

The two men straightened. One of them said through his mask, "If that Nabors fool hadn't got away, we'd have almost all the patients we need, now that we've got the girl."

The man holding the hypo nodded, said, "Let's get it over with." He started toward the place where Kane lay, followed by the other two.

Fred Kane went momentarily mad with fear in that second. For he knew now why he had been brought here—and he knew the meaning of that blood-filled hypodermic.

He was to be given the Green Death!

CHAPTER FOUR

DEATH IN HIS VEINS

KANE WRITHED like a snake against the ropes that held him. The skin tore loose and blood seeped into his palms, but he did not feel it. Exhausted, he went very still, his lips parted, cold; his eyes wide open and colorless.

He too would have the Green Death. There would be violent headaches for a day or so. His body would burn with fever. His skin would turn rotting green. He would go mad with pain, howl and writhe and fight to kill himself and end his misery. And all the while that he waited to go mad he would know what was coming—and be helpless to prevent it!

"I see he's conscious," a voice said.

Kane jerked his head, saw the three men staring down at him from over surgeon's masks. The words whipped his body into one last furious effort. The muscles in his arms and shoulders bulged like whipcord. Sweat broke out on his high forehead, ran down into his eyes and across ridged cheekbones. His fingers were hooked and stiff as steel talons. Blood oozed between them as the ropes dug into his twisting wrists. But the knots held.

For more than a minute he fought, lashed by wild terror until he was all but insane. If they had come to kill him outright he could have waited and smiled. But this disease, this thing that drove men crazy and rotted their flesh as they lay helples.... Finally Kane fell back exhausted. His mind was sodden, hopeless.

One of the men laughed. "He puts up as much fight beforehand as he will afterward."

"Let's get it over," the man with the hypo said. His voice was muffled by the mask, but Kane stiffened. Somewhere he had heard that voice before.

It took two men to hold Kane while the other injected the blood. Even so they were forced to strike him with the butt of an automatic. The blow didn't knock him entirely unconscious, but it seemed to break contact between his brain and muscles. He lay motionless, saw the bloodfilled hypo come close to his arm, felt the prick of the needle, saw the blood from the glass bowl slowly vanish into his vein.

The men stood up. "There'll be no need to observe him for the next few hours," the man with the hypo said. They went out of the room on the side opposite the dying man. There were iron bars beyond this curtain too, Kane noted, but the men made no effort to close the small door in them.

Complete consciousness returned to Fred Kane slowly. And with it came crawling, mind-eating horror. The blood in his body felt cold and slimy. It seemed to creep through his veins with small, scaly feet that made his skin pimple and the hair along his neck rise stiffly. From the room beyond came the dying man's screams, rolling over him in hoarse, choked notes.

He would be screaming like that soon.

Kane shuddered. He didn't know anything about medicine, but he knew that blood from the dying man's body would carry the germs of the disease. And now the germs were within his veins, coming closer to his mind like an army of rats ready to gnaw at his brain. Soon he would go mad! Mad, and screaming in agony.

"Oh God!" he said aloud. "Good God!"

Then he fought himself to calmness. His lips were thin and cold but they ceased to quiver; He'd faced death before—but this—God! He shuddered, caught his nerves in an iron will and made them steady again. He could take death when it came. There was nothing he could do for himself now. He had to die—in agony. But there was something he could do for the city. If he escaped from this place he could call the inspector, have a whole squad descend on these fiends who murdered men with disease.

He began a steady struggle against his bonds. The skin had

been rubbed from his wrists and the ropes ground on raw flesh. Kane's jaw set hard and he kept working. The exertion started blood flowing from the place the gun butt had landed. It oozed out of his matted black hair and down across his forehead. His lids were narrowed against the pain in his wrists until his grimy, blood-smeared face seemed an eyeless mask of horror.

His head was aching. Kane knew the pain came from the blow, yet he kept saying through cold lips, "It can't be the disease yet. Not yet!"

ONE, two hours slid by. The ropes bit deeper into his wrists, but the knots never slipped. A wild fury blew like a storm through Kane. He had to get loose! Had to! Otherwise these fiends would continue to capture persons, bring them into this hell-hole, and watch them die in agony.

Soon they would come back to watch him. Almost sick with pain he rolled over in a last wild effort. His blood and dirt caked hands bit at the ground—but the ropes held.

Kane went limp, exhausted. He was whipped. He couldn't beat these ropes. He lay breathing heavily, staring at the wall from which the gasoline lantern shed its fierce white glare.

Abruptly, then, he jerked himself to a sitting position. His lips curled back from his teeth and his eyes narrowed. "Damn it! There's a chance," he said.

Wriggling his knees under him, Fred Kane flung his body up and back, managed to stand erect. Hopping, he went across the dirt floor. The lantern was shoulder high, swung from a peg in the concrete. The floor beneath it was of dirt, but packed hard as rock.

Kane looked down at the floor, at the lantern again. Sweat and blood and dirt made a nightmare of his face; behind thin pulled lips his teeth showed strangely white. He sucked a long breath. From the next room the cries came steadily.

Well, it was better to burn, if the worst came, than to die of the Green Death. Stooping, he put his head under the lantern, straightened.

Light whirled about the room as the lantern fell. Kane tried to throw himself to one side, out of the way of the gasoline, should it explode. His bound ankles brought him smashing to earth, close beside the lamp.

It hit the floor with a crash. Blackness whipped through the room. Light glimmered yellow and red for a half second. Kane watched as a bird might watch a snake advancing.

The red light went out and there was pitch darkness in the room except for the thin white line beneath the left curtain. Kane rolled to the spot where the lantern had fallen, lay on his hip and began to grope with his fingers. The glass shade had broken but the heavy container for the gasoline hadn't. Tortured fingers found a jagged piece of glass....

Ten minutes later Fred Kane stood erect, working stiff, bloody fingers. He took several short, high steps, flexing the muscles of his legs. The men had gone to the right, not planning to return for several hours. That was probably the way out. Kane turned to the right.

It was ebony dark beyond the right curtain. Kane groped along the iron fence, found the gate and went through. The next room was like a sea of ink crowding against his eyes, seeming to clog his very lungs with darkness.

Kane started wading through the darkness, hands outstretched, feet sliding cautiously before him. He found another curtain, but no iron grating. Pushing by, he kept going. Another curtain, and there was a dull stirring in the darkness. Kane tensed, listening. The cries of the dying man were barely audible now, only a recurrent whispered horror in the blackess. Ahead there was nothing.

KANE started forward again. He passed another curtain and stopped sharply. Beyond a long pool of darkness was a white line—a light below the next curtain. A muffled voice floated through the gloom.

Sudden anger flamed in Fred Kane's body. His long fingers twitched, and were rigid. His breath came through clenched teeth. Here, just ahead, were the men who had killed him. Soon his body would be a living flame of agony without hope of anything save death. These same men had tortured others. Now....

Kane crossed the room like a stalking panther. Near the thin line that marked the curtain he went down on his hinds and knees. He caught the bottom of the curtain between bloody fingers, lifted it and peered under.

The room was lighted by a lamp hung on the right wall. A thick rug had been spread over the dirt floor. There were two beds, a dresser, two easy chairs, but the general shape of the room was the same as that in which Kane had stayed. In the middle of the room was a card table and at it two men were playing stud poker.

His fingers tightened on the drape, wrinkling it in tiny folds.

He didn't know these men, but he knew the type. Average height, thick-set, brutal. The slender man who had injected the blood into his arm was not here. Instinctively Kane knew that he was the central figure behind this whole fiendish business. But what could he possibly gain by such hellishness? Was he some madman playing with death in new and horrible forms?

One of the men at the table said, "Jack bets," and tossed out a chip.

The other called, said, "We better get back to that damn detective after this game. The boss'd raise hell if we missed the first things he does."

Kane's big shoulders stiffened. The slender man was probably in some room beyond this one. If Kane could hide while these men went back to look for him, he might be able to slip through.

He began to crawl toward the right wall.

His raw fingers slapped unexpectedly on a rock and pain shot through his arms. Before he could stop himself he said aloud, "Damn!"

A silence that crescendoed to a furious, intense and utter soundlessness struck the tunnel. For one second Fred Kane remained motionless on his hands and knees, mouth still open. Beyond the curtain the two gangsters sat staring at one another, immobile as a picture.

The tableau broke. Fred Kane scooped up the bottom of the curtain a half inch from the floor, peeped under. The two gangsters were whirling, coming out of their chairs, crashing them over, pulling guns as they moved. Both leaped toward the curtain.

THERE was no use of turning to dash back the way he had come. Kane was weak, still tired from the struggle against his bonds. Somewhere in that long tunnel they would overtake him. His only chance was to go forward.

Kane plunged headlong into the curtain. It billowed around him, flapped against his face, almost tripped him. A gun blasted and Kane felt the drape jerk as a bullet tore through six inches from his head. Another shot.

The cloth rippled back over Kane's face, his head, and was gone. The two gunmen were near the curtain and about the center of the room. Kane was far to the right. They were half crouched, bringing up their guns, slowly, confidently.

Kane's right hand lashed through the air, struck the gasoline lantern. The thing went whirling off the wall, spinning wildly. A gun roared. Kane staggered in his stride as the bullet ploughed a shallow trench across his chest.

The lamp crashed to the floor. Blackness roared through the room. Guns blasted and two tongues of flame spit into the darkness. Bullets struck the concrete wall, ricocheted, and shrieked into the darkness like banshees. Kane went ploughing through the curtain at the far side of the room.

Light struck his eyes again. Another lamp on the right. Directly ahead the room ended, a solid wall of concrete with two chains dangling, pulleys overhead. Behind him steps pounded. A half second and they'd be on him from the rear. In front his way was blocked.

Kane's eyes glittered at the pulleys. His flailing right hand caught the lamp and sent it crashing. Stygian dark opened its mouth and swallowed the room. He didn't stop running in time and his shoulder jarred hard against the concrete wall. He staggered backward, caught one of the chains, yanked.

Behind him guns roared in the tunnel, making wild shaking echoes. Bullets spanked the wall a few inches from his face. He heard the oiled sliding of the pulleys overhead. Gray light showed in front of him. He leaped headlong, his body tense, waiting for the bullet that would find him etched against the light.

There was a hoarse shout behind. "Don't shoot! They'll hear...

The gate's up!"

Fred Kane saw the train track a split second before his foot struck it. He pitched forward, hands beating at the air, clawing madly as though to hold himself erect.

For just in front of him as he fell was the electric rail!

He kept falling. Somehow he got his left foot under him, shoved. His body arched. He saw the rail come rushing at his head. Air tore in a gasp through his nostrils. Then he had cleared the charged rail, struck on the other side, rolled to his feet. He whirled, went racing down the subway tunnel.

Once he twisted his head and looked back. Nothing but solid, concrete walls.

HE slowed to a walk, pulling long, deep breaths into his lungs, letting them out until his chest ached. God! He was tired and his head was hurting. "It's from the blow," Kane said aloud. "It can't be the disease—yet."

He found suddenly that his fingers were trembling. While it had been men and guns that threatened his life he had been without fear. But now….

"God!" he said aloud. "I—I'll be spreading the disease!"

Would he give it to other persons merely by walking near them? He had to get out of here, call the inspector to send down a squad. He knew now that the disappearing men were being hidden in an abandoned subway tunnel that had been cleverly blocked off. No one would ever find them unless….

There were half a dozen persons on the subway platform. Beyond the turnstiles a faint light showed from the stairway. "Daylight," Kane said aloud. The clock on the change booth showed 6:12.

Even before Kane reached the platform he noticed the persons waiting there. Four of them had newspapers and were reading, but from time to time they would glance cautiously toward the person nearest. In every face there was fear—stark dread.

Probably there are more cases in the paper this morning, Kane thought. An epidemic, a plague…. And he himself carrying the germs. But he had to reach a telephone.

There was no one waiting at this end of the platform. Kane put his hands on it and tried to vault up. He was still weak and for a moment he hung swaying, legs dangling below the edge, head and shoulders above it.

A woman screamed in terror. The newspaper she had been reading fell rustling at her feet. She stood, mouth jerking, eyes wide, arm and finger pointed rigidly toward Kane. Then she whirled. The turnstile clattered as she raced through.

Chaos broke loose on the platform. Screams rang out from both the uptown and downtown sides; wild, jangling cries of fear that shrieked weirdly along the tunnel.

Men and women dashed for the turnstiles, clawed at one another, fought through and up the steps. Fred Kane hung there at the edge of the platform staring after them, wide eyed, amazed. What had terrified them? Was the whole city mad with fear?

He struggled onto the platform. As he did so he noticed his blood covered, grimy hands. He smiled thinly. His face must be as gruesome looking as his hands. The papers had probably carried stories about persons disappearing from this section. He picked up the paper the woman had dropped. Great black letters glared from the page.

GREEN DEATH STRIKES NINE MORE

Epidemic Feared; Police Think Victims
Snatched, Then Diseased

Subhead lines declared doctors were hopeless before the threat. It was possible that the Green Death might destroy New York as the plague had wiped out London in 1665. Several more patients had died. Death seemed positive once the disease was contracted....

FRED KANE'S fingers crushed the paper, leaving spots of dried blood. His mouth was pale against his dark face and a nerve under his right eye kept twitching. He was going to die—like the man he had seen in the hospital, like others, like the one he had seen back there in the abandoned tunnel, writhing in torture on the ground, screaming, crazy with pain. Going to die in agony, unable to fight.

"Oh, God!" he said aloud.

The tunnel rumbled to an oncoming train. The sound struck at Kane's fear-cold mind. Well, he wouldn't die before he'd turned those fiends over to the police. Suddenly he wondered where the green-faced men in the hoods had been while the others worked on him. The gunmen didn't have green faces.

He remembered sharply the hideous specter rising out of the ground—out of the grave itself. His teeth clamped on his lower lip to still its trembling.

There was a telephone booth inside the turnstiles and Kane stepped toward it. He raised a bloody hand and pushed it through dark hair. The rumble of the train was increasing his headache sharply. Kane's teeth dug deeper into his lip. It was just from the blow. It couldn't be the disease. It couldn't....

He stepped inside the telephone booth and pulled the door shut behind him. The train had stopped, but the air inside the booth seemed to be shaking with thunder and stiflingly hot. God! It was hot, but he wasn't sweating. He wondered why.

Dropping in a nickel he raised his finger to dial headquarters, stopped. What was the number? Hell, he knew that number as well as he knew his name. The pain in his head was becoming wild, furious. His left hand clenched the receiver, his right hand clawed at the box on the wall. This pain was driving him mad. He couldn't think, couldn't....

He caught himself up sharply. He had to think, had to remember that number. Let his nerves slip and he'd go insane. Had to keep control of himself.

He watched the forefinger of his right hand as though it were utterly detached from his body, as it moved toward the dial.

It dialed the operator and he heard himself asking for police headquarters. A moment later he was talking in short, broken syllables. The agony within him had become a wild fury, gnawing at his brain, crawling through his body like fire, searing his veins.

"This is Fred Kane," he said. "Missing Persons. Broadway subway, 157th Street.... Send a squad.... There're graves in the cemetery.... Things come out...." He couldn't say any more.

The fire in his body had burned the very air from his lungs. He stood clawing at the telephone, swaying. He could hear the man at the other end shouting questions, but the words made no sense. Kane gasped, "An ambulance—got—Green Death."

The receiver clattered from his hand. He swayed backward against the wall.

God but it was hot! The fire was inside and out. His head was bursting. He *had* to get more air. He pushed against the door of the booth, almost fell out when it opened. Rocking like a drunken man he started toward the stairway.

Two men and a policeman were standing at the foot of the steps watching him. One was the round-faced, bald-headed man from the change booth. His pink face seemed white with fear now, but there was another look in the narrow, glittering eyes. Curiosity? Hatred? Kane couldn't tell. He stood staring at the bald-headed man, his brain struggling for a pain-blurred thought. This man worked here where these things....

The policeman took a slow step forward. He was gripping his club hard. His face was drawn with terror. He said huskily, "All right. Who...?"

Kane made a gesture with his right hand. He couldn't control the muscles and it swung in wide. He said, "Keep crowd back—ambulance coming...."

God! He couldn't stand this torture any longer.

He pitched forward, hung like an empty sack across the turnstile.

CHAPTER FIVE

TWO DAYS TO LIVE

"*PUT HIM* on the stretcher and carry him up," a voice was saying.

Hands seemed to pick Kane out of the air. Someone said, "Cheeze! This guy's temperature must be 140."

"They always run a high temperature," the first voice said in its clipped, brisk fashion. "It'll go higher with each attack until he finally burns out and dies."

Kane felt himself floating through the air. The pain in his head wasn't so bad now. It still hurt and he still felt hot, but he was breathing easier.

When his eyes finally opened he was inside an ambulance. Dr. Charles Stuart was sitting beside the cot, watching him out of black, hawk eyes over a strong, hawk nose. "How are you feeling now?" he asked. His slim fingers found Kane's pulse.

Kane said, "Better. I'll be all right in a—"

He stopped, mouth still open. The attacks were recurrent, the doctors had told him yesterday. Each one would be worse than the one before until he went completely mad. Worse than the one he'd just had… God!

He twisted abruptly toward the doctor. "Did the cops get there? They find that old tunnel where the men were hidden?"

The hawk eyes narrowed. The slim fingers left his wrist to move upward and touch his forehead. "Just take it easy," Stuart said precisely. "The police came out, all right."

"Damn it!" Kane said. He knew what the doctor meant. "I'm

not out of my head now. That's where the persons go that disappear. I saw them. We've got to—"

Stuart shook his head. "Just keep quiet. You'll see some of the police at the hospital, if you want. You're still weak now."

INSPECTOR McFARLANE stood running his blunt fingers along his square jaw. "You just stay here and do as the doctors tell you," he said. "We'll take care of the other."

Kane clenched the side of the bed in desperation. He could see the disbelief in McFarlane's eyes. They all thought the disease had him out of his head and making up yarns about things that rose out of graves. They didn't believe his story about the empty tunnel.

"Dammit, Inspector!" Kane said. "I'm not crazy! I'm not!" His voice went high.

Dr. McGrath leaned forward. "You'll have to keep still," he said. "Otherwise you'll bring on the next attack sooner." He turned and with Stuart and McFarlane went out of the room, pulling the door shut behind them.

Kane rolled to a sitting position on the bed. His hands were clenched in the covers, his mouth straight, an ugly line of muscle along his jaw. Was he crazy already? He had seen that thing come out of the grave, hadn't he? He knew there was an abandoned tunnel opening on the subway, even if the police hadn't found it. They hadn't made much of a search, damn them. But maybe they were right. Maybe he was....

"No! No!" Kane said the words aloud. He wasn't crazy yet. Not yet!

He slid his feet off the bed, stood up and stepped to the door. From outside came the mutter of voices. He put his head to the panel.

McGrath was saying, "...why they wouldn't sell the body. I offered all the money I'll make in six months to let me work on it. How the hell are we ever going to learn anything?"

Stuart said in his brisk, precise tones, "Maybe the detectives will let us have his body. He'll be dead within two days."

McGrath's voice was deep, almost drawling. "By that time half the city may have this thing."

Behind the door Fred Kane, wearing white hospital pajamas, stood half crouched, muscles taut. For a moment the voices of the two physicians were lowered. Then Stuart said, "It's the same graveyard where the detective says he got knocked on the head, where the Nabors girl disappeared last night while trying to do some detective work of her own."

Footsteps padded away from the door.

For a full minute, Kane didn't move. So the Nabors girl had vanished. He remembered how she had looked yesterday: slim, curving, her face pale and beautiful with its frame of red hair. And the fiends had captured her.

"Damn it!" Kane's lips jerked in a snarl. If nobody would believe him, he'd go back there himself. He glared about the room searching for clothes. None here.

The second attack came more suddenly than the first. There were a few throbbed notes of warning under his skull. His flesh began to grow warm as though a great fire were blazing in the room, coming closer. The air seemed hot and thin in his lungs.

The throbbing under his head became steady, intense. It began to swell, to push out on his skull as though it would burst apart. The heat began to eat at his brain. Little tongues of fire within his head, devouring his mind—driving him crazy.

Kane reeled to the bed, fell on it. His fingers sank deep into the sheets, jerking, ripping the tough linen as though it had been paper. His teeth gripped the mattress, ground together. His body, writhed like that of a snake.

He did not hear the door open, the nurse's hurried call for the doctors. He did not see Stuart and McGrath watching him. He kept face down on the bed, fighting the agony as a man might fight against some wild beast that was ripping his body apart. Not once did Fred Kane cry out though he had split the sheets and torn plugs from the mattress before the pain subsided and he lay quietly, panting.

It was then that fear came to him again. "I've got to lie here," he thought, "and wait for this to happen again and again, getting worse. I've got to lie here until I go mad with torture."

He shuddered. While the pain lashed his body he had fought it, but now that it was gone there was nothing to do but wait—knowing that the same horror must come again. Nothing he could do would stop it. He had to lie there, waiting to die, waiting to be tortured.

"It's not the pain," he thought, "that drives them crazy. It's the waiting, waiting.... It'll get me again, and—" He choked a sob in his throat.

TWILIGHT showed gray and blue beyond the hospital window. Fred Kane lay staring at it. His brows were pulled straight above his eyes. He was going to die. Hope had gone out of him. But he wasn't going to lie here in this bed and die like a woman. The inspector hadn't believed the story Kane had told. He hadn't even investigated that pink-faced, bald-headed man in the subway change booth.

Kane's fingers tightened on the bed covers. He'd go back to that subway, that cemetery himself....

He lay very still, making plans. There was no chance of getting away in daylight wearing pajamas.

The wings of dusk beat thick about the windows when at last he stood up, stepped to the door. Cracking it open, he peered outside. The hall was empty. Directly across the hall was an elevator. On bare feet he slipped forward, pushed the button and raced back for his room. He stood gripping the door, watching, praying he wouldn't have another attack before he could get out.

No one passed in the hall. The light showed over the elevator; the door slid open and the Negro boy looked out.

It took Kane four steps to cross the hall. The boy saw him coming and his mouth jerked open in terror, his eyes went wide and rolling. So they all knew who he was, Kane thought.

The boy tried to cry out. The scream half stuck in his throat. Then Kane's fist landed on the boy's chin. The Negro pitched backward. His head and shoulders struck the side of the elevator and he slid to a sitting position. Kane had the door shut, the elevator started before the boy touched the floor.

Kane went to the basement, pulled the door open and looked

out. No one around. The elevator boy was still unconscious. Kane glanced at him, cursed. Trying to get into those clothes would be worse than wearing the pajamas. He went out of the basement on the trot.

He hailed a taxi, climbed in. The driver turned to stare at him, wide-eyed. The detective said, "Get going and keep your eyes front...."

At his apartment, Kane told the driver to wait. There was a chance he'd give the driver the disease. He didn't like that, but it was better to have one take the risk than several. He had to get out to that cemetery and subway!

Kane put on a blue double-breasted suit, hung another police special under his armpit, went out and crawled in the taxi again. "Broadway and 155th Street—the cemetery," he said.

The moon was full and still low in the east. As they turned at 155th Street, the hedge about the cemetery was a dark blot against the silvered darkness of the grass beyond. The tombstones showed white and ghostly.

The driver pulled his head around to look at Kane. He was a small man with big eyes, thin hair. "Where'bouts out here, sir?" There was nervousness in his tone.

Kane said, "Right here." He looked at the meter. It said $4.45. Kane got out, turned to the driver. "You married?"

The man shook his head.

"All right," Kane said. "You take the rest of the night off. Don't pick up any more fares. And take tomorrow off. Stay by yourself. If you start getting bad headaches, call the Medical Center. Tell 'em exactly what happened tonight." He tossed a fifty-dollar bill through the window.

The driver caught it, looked at it. The big eyes spread all over his small face. "Hell, boss," he said. "I don't mind a headache."

Kane said, "You'll mind that one." He pulled another bill from his pocket, asked, "You going to stay *alone?* Get me? See nobody."

"Sure."

Kane tossed him the money. "I won't have any need for it," he said bitterly. He turned on his heel and went toward the cemetery....

ONCE inside the hedge, Kane picked a cautious way through the graves. He moved slowly, keeping hidden as much as possible, eyes sweeping the moon-washed slopes about him. He didn't have any definite plan, but he wanted to look the place over. He couldn't forget the hideousness of that Thing rising out of the very ground behind him, out of a grave, perhaps. Thinking of the Thing made Kane feel cold along his back.

Abruptly he remembered the caretaker, Ike Neganzi. Last night the man had tried to shoot him. A few minutes later someone, some Thing, had risen out of the ground to attack Kane. Persons had disappeared both inside the cemetery and near it. Years ago Neganzi had sworn to make the City of New York suffer for his prison term. Could he...?

Still keeping low, Kane started toward the caretaker's house.

He had entered the cemetery by one of the end gates. To reach Neganzi's, he had to pass close by the place where he had been struck the night before.

He was within fifty yards of the point when he saw the shadow, saw its swaying, rhythmic movements.

Kane froze, half crouched behind a tombstone, eyes straining against the semidarkness. Moonlight washed most of the cemetery, but straight ahead four tall cedar shrubs were set in a square, and within the dark shadows between them Kane saw the man move, and vanish.

Keeping tombstones between himself and the cedars, Kane began to slip forward. He had gone twenty yards when he heard the soft *chunk, chunk* that came from the shadows. He edged forward.

Chunk. Chunk.

The sound came again, then stopped. Kane's lips pulled thin. He recognized that sound now. A spade striking soft earth. Kane's right hand went under his coat, came out again holding the gun.

The strain of staring into the darkness was beginning to make his eyes ache and a little pain was growing just back of the right one. Sudden fear lashed him like a whip. God! He couldn't have an attack now—just as he was about to catch the man.

He wouldn't.

Kane came to his feet with a surge, leaped toward the cedars. His breath was harsh in his nostrils, the gun hard against his hip. In the shadows something whirled, sprang....

CHAPTER SIX

PASSAGE TO HELL

KANE'S LEFT arm brushed the cedar as he went by. Straight in front of him was a mound of earth, a dark pit.

Beyond that a man leaped for the trees.

"Stop!" The word burst from Kane's lips. His finger curled hard around the trigger.

The man halted, turned slowly. His face was almost invisible in the shadows. Kane had skidded to a stop at the side of the pit. He looked down, caught a sharp breath. It was a new grave. Heaps of wreaths and cut flowers were piled at one end.

The pain in his head was growing rapidly. He set his teeth hard, stared across the open grave at the man beyond. "Take a step to the right," he said.

The man moved slowly. Moonlight tipped the cedar and fell on his face. Small eyes peered out from behind rimless glasses above a button nose. Kane said, "Dr. McGrath!"

The doctor caught a sharp breath, leaned suddenly forward. "You! What are you doing here?"

Kane's teeth were grinding together against the agony that was growing steadily. Fear was coming with the pain this time. Was this the attack that would drive him insane? He pushed words through clenched teeth. "What are you doing here, digging in graves?"

The doctor hesitated and Kane saw fear leap swiftly in his face. Kane snapped, "Talk, damn you! Quick!" He had to talk quickly or else Kane couldn't hear him. God! He *was* going mad!

McGrath's voice was still slow, but the insulting note was gone. "One of the victims was buried here. I wanted his body to study. But—" He paused and his next words seemed to come like salamanders through the flame that lashed Kane's body— "The grave was empty!"

Kane staggered. The whole world was whirling in a mist of fire.

Across the grave McGrath moved without warning. His body flickered into the shadows, vanished. Kane lunged blindly forward. His foot struck the heaped earth and he went headlong. The blackness of the grave came up at him. Then he was in it.

Kane felt his body strike the earth—and then, *oh, God, he was falling through the earth, falling into hell.* His whole body was afire with agony and he went flaming like a meteor through darkness.

THE next half hour was a frenzied blur of tortured action to Fred Kane. Occasional fleeting thoughts beat their way through the flame that roared within his body. Now and then the idea came to him that he was crazy, a raving maniac, frothing at the mouth, staggering, reeling with pain.

He never knew exactly when his fall ceased or when he staggered to his feet.

Once he thought dully that it was strange he was walking. He had fallen into an open grave—and kept falling, falling.... Now he was reeling through darkness. "Walking the path to hell," he sobbed aloud.

He never saw the thread of light. He never heard the screams that shuddered through the darkness, wailed, fading into moaning sobs along the tunnel. He did not know that he still gripped the .38 special in his hand. He never saw the curtain until he blundered into it, thrust it aside and stood in the glare of the lantern.

Then he saw only dimly, and for a second the sight made no impression on his pain-soaked mind.

It was a room like the others he had seen in the abandoned subway. Crouched against the wall was a girl. Her clothes were half torn from her, and he could see her left breast rising and falling, milk-white against the blue dress. Around her face and over her shoulders red gold hair fell like a storm.

It was the girl he had met in the hospital—Rose Nabors!

Directly in front of her, reeling toward her, was a man. His face was green as scum over stagnant water. Saliva drooled nastily from his mouth. His hands were extended clawlike toward her. Kane could see the long scarlet streak starting at the base of her throat and running down between her breasts where fingers had clawed once before.

On the far side of the room were three men wearing surgeon's masks and gowns. Two of them carried big sticks.

Kane saw these things through the wall of fire that blazed between his eyes and brain. He knew that the man in the center had the green death, would soon die of it.

And those fiends were killing her as surely as they were murdering him, with the disease.

The green man reeled toward the girl. His eyes were jerking insanely. His hands were almost at her throat and she cringed sideways along the tunnel, face twisted with horror.

A masked man shouted, stabbed with his left arm toward Kane. His right hand jerked the heavy stick back, hurled it.

KANE did not feel the wind as the stick whipped past his face. More by instinct than by reason he was pulling up the gun, leveling it, muzzle centered on the lunatic.

The girl screamed as fingers touched her throat, clawed. Kane heard the roar of his gun, barely conscious that he fired. He saw the insane man stagger, clap both hands to his left side, and fall.

The masked men were wrestling clumsily, gloved hands under the surgeons' gowns. The girl stared at Kane for one second, her mouth open, eyes round. Then she turned and leaped through the curtain on the far side.

Rubber-gloved hands were coming from under white gowns now. Kane saw the glint of blue steel. Again more by instinct than any thought within his agony-torn brain he acted. He leaped forward at the curtain, trying to swing his gun around. The curtain brushed over him, shutting out the light. A gun roared and a bullet spanked concrete, went wailing along the tunnel.

Kane jumped backward again. His foot slipped and he went

down hard. There was nothing but darkness now, not even a crack of light to mark the curtain. They must have extinguished the lantern, he thought dully.

A red tongue licked like a snake's and vanished. Thunder rolled through the subway. Kane squeezed the trigger of his gun, felt it shake in his hand. The world was breaking into splintering roars. Red fingers stabbed at him.

He knew he wouldn't last much longer. The pain had him now. He was going out in a minute. Going mad… mad….

Something struck his left shoulder, twisting him in the dirt. He knew that a bullet had hit him, but it felt no more than a jar compared with the torture of the disease.

He heard his gun boom again, saw fire spit back at him. Within his body the blaze lashed high; it snatched at his mind, tore at it. He screamed….

HIS body was a charred ember, cooling into dead ashes. Perhaps he was dead now and there would be no more torture.

But even now there was pain. A dull, far-off aching. He moved restlessly and the pain stabbed a sudden finger through his body. It brought full consciousness.

He was lying in utter darkness, flat on his face. His left shoulder was hurting and his coat felt oozy, sticky.

Kane got weakly to his feet. With his right hand he pulled matches from his pocket, struck one. The light was yellow and flickering in the darkness. It showed a dirt floor, a dark, ugly stain where his shoulder had been. He held the match close to his coat. It was blood-soaked. There was a round hole just above the armpit.

The match burned Kane's fingers and he dropped it, struck another. The flame glittered on the barrel of his revolver. Still holding the match, he picked up the gun with the same hand, dropped it in his coat pocket.

He found the curtain, pushed it aside. He went across this room and another, wondering why those masked fiends had not killed him. Perhaps they had thought him dead. And the green-faced ghouls he had seen in the subway and the cemetery, what had happened to them?

He had gone perhaps a hundred yards when he heard a voice. His hand tightened around the butt of his gun, his eyes squinted. He didn't have much more time to settle accounts with these devils.

It was hard to walk without making noise. His knees were weak and he fought to make them steady. The voices were closer now. He saw a light close to the floor.

Kane almost laughed. Crazy, insane joy started with the pain in his shoulder and surged up through his head. One more curtain and he'd be at them. He'd kill them like snakes.

His gun muzzle touched the curtain. He flung it aside and lunged through.

He stopped suddenly, eyes growing wide in his face, body rocking. A half dozen policemen had spun, guns ready.

Now he knew why the masked killers had not made sure he was dead. The girl had escaped, called the police.

There was horror in the faces of the men who stared at Kane. He knew some of them. McDougald, Nelson, Ricca. But not one of them was moving toward him, not one had spoken. Then a lantern-jawed detective raised a bony finger, pointing it at Kane's face.

"Good God!" the man said. "It's Fred Kane. And his face is—green!"

The weakness flooded up from Kane's knees through his whole body. He went down slowly until he sprawled in the dirt.

CHAPTER SEVEN

WAITING FOR MADNESS

"*NOT MUCH* to this shoulder wound," Dr. Stuart said as he finished the bandage. He turned to the square-faced man beside the bed, snapped, "You'll have to talk fast, Inspector. He'll have another attack soon. He'll need a strait-jacket before that." The hawk-faced doctor went out of the room.

Dr. McGrath stood gripping the foot of the bed until his finger-nails showed white. His eyes glinted behind their spectacles.

The police inspector looked down at Kane, said, "Now tell me all you know about this thing."

In tumbling words, Kane told him. The story seemed weird, fantastic even now.

"I-I fell into the grave," Kane said. "I don't know how I got into the tunnel."

"We've checked that," McFarlane said. "The grave had been robbed from beneath. That abandoned tunnel runs under part of the cemetery. Probably that's the way you were carried in the first time. They escaped and evidently took several of their victims with them. But they were rushed and left a couple."

How about the girl, Kane said. It was strange how much he had thought about her.

McFarlane grunted. "She says she was caught while walking near the cemetery, early this morning. She was held all day by two men, and not bothered until the third one came. That was just a few minutes before you got there." He turned his big square face toward McGrath. There was a brittle tone in his voice when he said, "You notified us of your escape with Kane *after* the girl called. If you were going to tell us, why didn't you do it sooner? We might have reached Kane in time to join in the fight."

The doctor's hands tightened on the bed. He spoke slowly, "I—I ran away from the cemetery. I knew the penalty for disinterring bodies. I thought I'd run away. I was frightened. After I began to think, I knew I couldn't get away, so I called you."

Dr. Charles Stuart came back into the room. An assistant followed him carrying a heavy, full-length strait-jacket. Together they began to strap it on Kane. It hurt when they slipped his wounded arm through the sleeves. His lips were caught hard between his teeth. His face was a pale green.

Through Kane's mind flashed a picture of the other man he'd seen wearing a strait-jacket and lying on a hospital bed—crazy with pain. That man had died five hours ago. Kane's nostrils quivered as he sucked a breath. So he was going mad now—mad.... He'd howl and writhe like those others had done. How long would it take him to die? How long would he have to lie in agony?

HE shook his head savagely, asked, "How about the girl, Doc? You think she's got...?"

"I don't know yet," Stuart said. "Very likely...."

He finished strapping the strait-jacket, rolled Kane over on his back.

Straight, as unemotional as a hawk, Stuart gazed down at the detective. "Anything else you want to say?"

Kane shook his head.

McFarlane's big jaw waggled. Kane saw him swallow, blink his eyes furiously. The inspector reached out a big hand, tapped Kane on the shoulder. "So long." He almost choked.

Kane said, "So long, Chief." His lips shut tight. His jaw muscles bulged. He knew what this good-bye meant. It was his last one. Within a few hours he'd be insane—and soon... dead.

McFarlane turned toward McGrath. "You come with me for a while," he said.

Stuart nodded to his assistant. The man bent, taped Kane's

mouth. Kane could feel the tape pulled hard across his thin lips, across his jaw. He started to shake his head, swear that nothing could make him cry out. Then he stopped, remembering the way he had screamed in the subway.

Stuart switched off the light. The doctors and McFarlane went out of the room. The door shut behind them.

Fred Kane lay flat on his back, unable to move except for his eyes, waiting. Waiting for insanity.

His eyes were green in a green face now. They were twitching nervously. He tried to keep them still. "I'll look at the window and nothing else," he thought. It was a white-silled window, big and deep. Outside there was darkness. He was on the second floor, he remembered.

His eyes twitched away from the window, around the dark room. Kane's mind began to race, to beat at his skull. He couldn't lie here like a tied animal and wait for death. He wanted to get up and struggle for life. Waiting, that was what drove them crazy. God! He couldn't wait!

He tried to jerk himself erect, failed. His body jerked, rolled half on one side, fell back.

He tried to scream. He wanted to tell them he didn't mind the pain, but God! he couldn't lie here this way. Waiting... waiting.... Soon he'd be mad! Why....

Kane clutched at his nerves, fought them to stillness. "You're turning yellow," his tongue said, though there was no sound. "That's what takes guts. Just to lie still. Even a rat can fight if it has to. But can you take it this way?

"I'll soon be mad. I'll soon be mad." The words kept beating through his mind. It wasn't death he dreaded lying here. It was the horrors that had to come before he could die....

The maddening pain came swiftly....

KANE did not know when the agony began to recede, but hours later the fire went out of his head. His eyes opened. There was the pale white of the wall showing through the darkness. He followed it around, found the lighter rectangle that was the night-cloaked window.

In the gray rectangle of the window was appearing a figure, like the black cloud of a cyclone forming against a slate-gray sky. The whole room swayed in his fevered gaze, and the thing in the window swayed—and grew larger.

It was the hooded man from the subway! And Kane knew that beneath that hood was a green face!

The man slid soundlessly through the window. He stepped to one side and almost vanished in the deeper darkness. Another began to show in the window.

Fevered, weird thoughts hurled through Kane's mind. Why had these things come for him? They had not come to the other victims in the hospital. Was he going to be one of them—grave-haunted ghouls who roamed in darkness beneath the earth, their bodies always racked by pain, their only desire to make others share that agony?

The second one slipped through the window. Side by side like to vultures they moved toward the bed. Kane's body was a mad lashing of immovable muscles within the strait-jacket.

The men paused beside him. Green fingers reached out and clenched on his shoulders, pulled them from the bed. The other slipped something about Kane's waist. He was lifted and carried toward the window.

Kane felt the window-sill beneath his feet. His body was pushed stiff as a board across it. His feet tilted downward. Far above he could see the dark and lighted windows, the dark line that marked the top of the building. Above that stars were pale, jittery spots in a blue-black sky.

Then he was swaying at the end of a rope, being lowered slowly. To his left he could see the ladder on which the hooded men had come.

From the blackness of the wall below him a third figure detached itself. Kane had been lowered into the drive and close by an ambulance was waiting. The figure caught him as his feet touched the pavement, held him erect. The rope piled around him as it was dropped from above.

A moment later the figures came down the ladder, slipped it inside the ambulance. Kane was lifted, thrust head first after the ladder. It was too dark to see plainly, but in the deep stillness he could hear breathing. Kane tensed, listening. It was the hushed, shallow breathing of fear.

Two of the men followed him into the rear of the ambulance. The door shut softly. The motor purred. The big car slid down the drive like a shadow.

"We did it," a man said.

The other said, "I hope we get there before he begins his next fit. It is probable that he will never recover consciousness once it starts. He should be mad for one or two days, then die."

KANE'S nostrils flared as he breathed. So! The next was the last. Well, he was glad. The sooner he went mad the better. Perhaps then the pain would cease. Something clogged in his throat, for he knew—the pain would never end until he died. The man in the subway had been mad, and screaming.

The other man asked, "What about the girl?"

"It's just beginning to affect her."

The ambulance passed a street light and Kane's eyes flickered to the left, watched the light filter through the window, run the length of the car, and vanish. In that split second he saw the person across from him.

It was Rose Nabors, bound and gagged!

Air tore from Kane's lungs. Why had she, too, been taken from the hospital? Was she also to be made one of the fiends?

Before the ambulance stopped, Kane's body was a living, jerking bundle of fire in which floated strange and horrible images.

Green-faced monsters were bending over him, lifting him. A pale white sea of moonlight swam round and round while through it red fires lashed out to strike his body. Around him wavering white tombs rose from a black, silver-coated earth.

Kane knew that he was mad now. He could hear terrific, throat-tearing screams that began deep in his belly, rose like flame through his chest, shattered his throat and burst within his brain, while his tongue thrashed soundlessly.

A tombstone stuck crazily into the whirling fire that was the air. Below the headstone an empty grave yawned blackly. Into the grave sank a green-faced, hooded terror and in his arms he carried Rose Nabors. Her body was a curving sweetness beneath the white gown.

The crazy tombstone was moving—or Kane was moving. He was swimming through the furious, jagged and horrible air, closer to the grave. He could see the lettering on the headstone.

Joshua Hawkes

Died of the Pestilence

1783

Insane laughter hurled up through Kane's belly where his very bowels were being ripped, and burst against his teeth. "Died of the Pestilence! Pestilence!"

IT was over, over at last and the sweet hand of death had cooled the fire in his body. There was no pain now, only an intense and utter weakness, a weak desire to lie still forever here in the grave into which he had descended.

Through the soft, cool darkness words came slowly. And Fred Kane realized, with shuddering revulsion, that he was still alive. That meant more torture....

The words came more distinctly. "He'll live, but keep your masks on. I'm not yet positive how the disease is transmitted and he may yet be contagious. But I've got the cure, and I'll get the reward money. That $100,000 will be just a drop in the bucket compared to what this does for my reputation. My notes are complete as to the cure and ready for inspection."

"Did you know it was going to work out like this?"

"Of course not. A great deal of science is trial and error. That's why I needed specimens to work on and hired you two to get them. I knew how these persons had contracted the disease, and I didn't know about the ones at the hospital. That's why I had to keep an eye on them.

"But since they had told the hospital doctors what had happened, I had to get them away or everyone would have known as much as I did."

Kane's eyes came open slowly. For a long while he gazed around vacantly. At last it focused. He was in another of the subway rooms, but one well furnished. He was lying on a cot. The strait-jacket still held him but the gag had been removed. Near him were three men wearing surgeons' masks that covered all but the eyes.

One of them leaned toward Kane. "So at last you are conscious," he said.

Kane nodded a feeble answer. Every muscle in his body was aching and sick.

"You've proved a great contribution to science," the masked man said. "I thought I was giving you the Green Death when I injected the blood. I've discovered I was giving you a toxin against it—as in the case of typhoid, smallpox and other diseases. Only I overdid your dose and instead of building up resistance in you, I almost killed you. But you'll live."

One of the other men said, "Hell, you ain't gonna let him go, are you, Chief?"

The man laughed. "I mean the disease won't kill him. Of course we'll have to dispose of him."

"The girl too?"

"The girl too."

Kane's voice was weak, yet eager. "She's alive?"

"Yes. I used the toxin on her as soon as I saw you had a chance. She's doing splendidly."

"It's tough we gotta shoot her," one of the men said. "She's too damn good-lookin'."

The brow of the slim man knitted. "I'm a bit worried about shooting them. Of course it's not likely that this section of the tunnel will ever be discovered. It's completely on the other side of the cemetery from the one that was found. But there's always a chance. And even skeletons may be identified. That might lead to...." He waved a gloved hand.

"How you gonna get rid of 'em?"

For a moment the man did not answer. Then his eyes smiled. "I have it. We'll dissolve them. You shoot them, then we'll dump the bodies in acid. When that's done...." He paused and the heavy-set man began to reach under his surgeon's gown, fumbling for a gun.

Kane's teeth clenched on his lower lip until warm blood spurted. He'd won through hell, only to die again, as helpless to fight as he had been against the disease. If he could only be alone for awhile there was one slim chance.... But if he failed, he brought more torture on himself and the girl.

His voice was hard in his throat when he said, "Listen, you claim I've been a contribution to science. I'd like one more chance at it. I've had every pain in hell these last few days. After all that I don't want to go out with a bullet. I want to fight to the end and if there's anything I haven't been through—" He tried to laugh, but the sound choked in his throat—"it's a tub of acid. I—I'd like to go into that, still fighting."

Above the white mask the eyes bored down at him. The squat man had the gun in his hand but was staring amazedly at Kane. He said, "You damn fool!"

The other said thinly, "A masochist, huh?" He hesitated. Kane lay staring up at him, not knowing whether he hoped the man would consent or refuse. There was one chance, but such a small one!

The man said abruptly, "Very well. I'd rather like to have you live a while longer anyway. I want to see if there is any reaction after the disease. Besides, it will take us some little while to get things ready. I'll have you fed and you may talk to the girl. The dying man's last wish, you know." The eyes above the mask glittered. "Eat, drink, and be merry," he quoted, "for tomorrow—you die."

CHAPTER EIGHT

ONE LAST DEATH

MINUTES PASSED while Fred Kane lay very still within the strait-jacket. Blood, thin, cold water within his veins. It seemed to drain away from his heart, leaving that cold and empty and dead.

The food which was brought tasted flat in his mouth, but he ate. Afterwards his body felt stronger, but inside he was hollow, dead. He tried to wriggle his left shoulder, found that the muscles ached less when they moved. Despite the disease the wound had healed slightly.

Then the girl was brought in. She too was on a cot, her slim body held by a strait-jacket. She was placed about fifteen feet from Kane.

The lean man said, "Tony, you stay here and keep an eye open. We'll be back when we can make it." He and one of the gunmen went out. Tony eased his broad frame into a chair near the wall.

Fred Kane rolled his head, looked at the girl on the next cot. She was watching him out of wide-spaced blue eyes. Her hair was loose and fell in a red gold heap upon the pillow. Her skin was as pale as a cape jasmine and there were dark lines under her eyes.

Sudden fury whipped the blood through Kane. His jaw teeth grated as he clenched them. They couldn't kill this girl! He had lain still waiting for his own death, but now his muscles began to twitch, his brain to roll furiously.

The girl saw the sudden convulsing of his face. Her eyes darkened. "What is it?" she asked.

Kane said, "Hello." It was all he could think of to say. It sounded insane and he cursed himself for an idiot. But he mustn't let her know for an instant what they were waiting for.

The gunman in the chair said, "Have your talk now. When the chief comes back you'll have to quit. For good."

A nerve quivered in the dark circle under her right eye. Her lips set firmly. Even they were pale, Kane noted. Otherwise she gave no indication of hearing the man's words. She said to Kane, "I—I appreciate you saving me a few days ago."

Kane's mouth twisted. He started to say a hell of a lot of good it had done, and stopped.

He asked, "Have you seen any more of the green faced men who brought us here? They seem to vanish."

She nodded slightly, making the red hair quiver. "These are the ones. They must wear the green on their faces to frighten anyone who sees them."

For the next hour or two they talked lightly. There wasn't much to say—waiting for death. Kane's mind kept reeling, searching for some means of escape. If only he could get out of this strait-jacket But the guard, sitting grimly at the other end of the room, was watching.

The girl dozed. Later Kane dropped into a fevered sleep.

HE awoke with a start. The three men were in the room once more. The slim one turned, looked at him over the surgeon's mask. "So you are awake," he said. "Well, we're ready." He nodded to the other two.

They lifted Kane from his cot, carried him beyond the green curtain that formed the left end of the room. Here the floor was dirt. The glow of one lantern extended down the tunnel and faded into darkness. Kane was carried through a small hole in the right side of the wall, dropped on the floor. The room was very small, concrete walled except for the thick wooden door through which he had entered. Almost the entire room was occupied by a huge glass tub filled with a clear, water-like liquid. From the right wall a rope ran up to a pulley in the center of the roof, dangled down above the tub.

The slim man said, "It took us a little while to get this ready, but it should leave no trace of you." While he talked the two gunmen went out, returned with the girl. "This was probably intended as an emergency exit when they thought the subway would run through this tunnel. It'll be an emergency exit for your souls. I've nearly a hundred gallons of *aqua regia* in that tub." He turned toward Tony, said, "Fetch that last corpse and we'll make a demonstration."

Kane rolled his head to look at the girl. They had stretched her near the left wall. Her blue eyes were wide, dark pools in her pale face. Her lips were sucked in and gripped by her teeth, but Kane could see the corners of them twitching. He wanted to scream, to shout aloud against this horror, but his voice choked in his throat. What good would it do to plead with men gone mad?

Tony returned carrying the body of a man in his arms. The corpse was green skinned, the limbs twisted from the convulsion in which this man had died. The mouth was open, dried saliva made nasty marks across the chin and throat.

"We've put in the others," the slim man said. "Watch this."

Tony lifted the corpse. He slid the feet over the edge of the thin glass tub, lowered the body till all but the head was submerged.

Kane's head jerked up from the floor, and his breath was like hot knives in his nostrils, ripping into his lungs. He heard the girl scream, a short, choked cry that broke into a whimper.

The body was clothed only in underwear when it slid into the acid. As Kane watched the cloth disappeared. The green flesh corroded, burst, and vanished. Below the ghastly, snarling head which Tony held by its brown hair a skeleton came into view. And slowly the bones became pockmarked, crumbled.

The slim man said, "That'll do." Tony released the head and it slid under the liquid. The face began to vanish.

"And now," the man said, "we'll have the last step. We'll swing you," he nodded almost pleasantly at Kane, "by the pulley." He turned to where a shelf on the wall jutted over the rope that ran to the pulley. There was a retort and a small tube on the shelf. "This will drop acid on the rope by which you hang. That'll give us time to get out of here and shut the door. When the acid eats the rope you'll fall. The tub is very thin glass. You'll hit one edge and break it. The acid will make a puddle a foot deep throughout the room. After some time it will sink into the ground. But before that," he gestured with his hand, "you'll be only a memory."

The next few minutes were a blurred haze in Kane's mind. Through his own curses he heard the girl sobbing quietly. He fought like a maniac against the strait-jacket, tried to twist his head and bite the hands of the men that lifted him. But in less than a minute the rope had been tied about his waist and he was dangling in the air, directly over the tub's edge.

On the floor below him the girl was crying in terror. The slim man said, "Well, good luck." He and the gunmen went out. The door shut behind them.

Terror was a giant wind that whipped Kane's body. His muscles beat like uncoiling springs against the strait-jacket—and ceased. Black horror stormed through his body.

SOMEHOW he fought his mind to calmness. It was possible to escape from a strait-jacket, if a man thought about it. It was when a man was crazy that a strait-jacket was impossible to remove. While waiting for the others to return he'd remembered seeing Houdini do it once, but there had been no chance with the guard watching. Now there was a chance—a very little chance.

He twisted his head, looked down. Acid was falling drop by drop from the retort to the rope. The rope would hold perhaps five more minutes.

Kane began a struggle that wrenched and tore every muscle of his body. As a boy he'd seen Houdini pull this trick. The idea was to get the right hand under the left elbow, then push that elbow up and over his head until both hands were in front of him. After that he could reach the straps, even if his hands were encased in the sleeves.

He got the fingers of his right hand under his left elbow, began to push. The wound in his shoulder burned like a hot brand. He cursed savagely, kept trying.

Drop by drop the acid fell. Two more minutes....

God! He had both hands in front of him now. His fingers were clumsy under the stiff canvas. He tried to clutch the straps and they slipped away from him. He got one loose and a finger showed. He pawed at the other.

The acid fell drop by drop. Frayed strands of rope twisted back from the half eaten section.

One hand burst loose. Kane jerked it over to clutch the other straps. The girl screamed.

Rolling, white-balled, Kane's eyes found the rope again. It seemed to be stretching, splitting. Too late—

Kane's free hand shot up, caught the rope above his head, and jerked. It made his body shiver, swung his feet outward. At the same instant the last strand broke. Kane plunged downward!

The acid seemed to rush toward him. The thin glass side of the tub. He screamed.

Then he was lying on the earth beside the tub, panting. That jerk on the rope had flung him just beyond the glass edge. He lay there feeling sick at his belly, the air hard and bulky in his nostrils. At last his breathing was easy and his left hand loosed the remaining straps. He climbed out of the strait-jacket, freed the girl.

The odds were still three to one. But the sense of terror was gone from Fred Kane. It was man to man now.

When the door was pushed open Kane could hear voices from the curtained room. His mouth broke into a smile. He stuck his head through the door, looked up and down the tunnel. To his right a gasoline lantern flung a brilliant glow. Beyond that was the heavy curtain. To the left the tunnel dwindled off into darkness.

Kane stepped through the doorway, paused. There was a dark shadow twenty feet down the tunnel and he went toward it cautiously. It was a rock the size of his fist. He picked it up.

Moving on the balls of his feet he went back to the lantern. Quietly he removed it from the wall. He stepped into the small room with the acid tub, extinguished the light, and emptied the gasoline. Holding the container carefully, he filled it with the acid.

ROSE NABORS was standing near the door. Her blue eyes

were large and frightened in her face, her hands tight pressed against her breasts. Kane's mouth was boyish when he grinned at her, even more so when he leaned and kissed her. Turning he went into the tunnel.

A white streak of light showed beneath the curtain. Kane held the acid-filled lamp in his left hand, the rock in his right. He caught the curtain with his left, tossed it aside and stepped through.

All three men had their backs turned, but they heard the rustle of the curtain and spun. Kane flung the rock. It hit Tony full in his snarling face and hurled him backward.

The man in the center was Dr. Stuart. His slim body was moving like a streak of shadow, diving for Kane's legs. The detective flung the acid. It was a silver spray in the light, slashing Stuart's face. The doctor screamed, fell in a writhing mass.

Beyond Stuart the gunman was digging furiously under his white gown. Even as Kane leaped forward, the man's hand flashed into view. Light glinted on the blue steel of an automatic. The gun swung upward.

Kane's left hand still held the empty lantern base. The bullet wound in his shoulder was aching, but his right hand was coming up from the hip, fast. The sound of it meeting bone mingled with the roar of the gun. The squat man went over backwards, struck on his right shoulder, rolled face down and lay motionless. He still held the gun in his hand. Kane stooped and took it from the unconscious fingers.

"Are—are you hurt?" It was the girl close behind him. He turned and her hands trembled at his chest.

Kane grinned. His eyes were bright and smiling in his dark face. Lord! The girl was pretty with her red hair towsled about her shoulders. Kane said, "Not hurt so I won't get over it."

She was very close to him. He could smell the fragile odor of her hair. He had walked in the shadow of death, but he was alive now and the world was for the living. She asked, "But why—why has the doctor done all this?"

Kane said, "He needed human beings to experiment with. Somehow he learned about this abandoned subway so he hired these men to kidnap persons and bring them here where he could work on them. He hoped to get a cure and collect the $100,000 reward. But it was the fame that he really wanted. It would have been worth more than the reward."

"But will the other doctors be able to cure the disease?"

"They will when I give them Stuart's notes. He said he'd kept a complete record. That'll put a stop to any epidemic."

Her mouth looked very soft and warm. Kane stopped slowly, saying, "The doctors will put an end to it for the others, but for me it's just beginning."

"What?"

He saw that she already understood, but he told her—in the proper way.

THE END

WYATT BLASSINGAME

WE DANCED WITH DEATH!

PERHAPS IT would have been better if I had died as the others did. Rats may gnaw on a corpse, maggots may crawl through it, and the dead do not object. But I live with the vermin of memory eating their way through my brain.

Looking back, I know that it really started that fall twilight in New Orleans. At the time I thought it a rather dangerous but interesting experience and nothing more. One never recognizes the minor events on which life hinges until they are beyond changing.

It was Bill Farlan who pulled the wires to get us into the *Varishti* meeting. We had heard something about the *Varishti* because their meeting place was in the block where McDonald intended to build his plant. Bill Farlan was the publicity man on the job and thought it would make a good story for us to attend that meeting. Neither McDonald nor Rogers had wanted to go, but Farlan had argued. So we all went, McDonald, Rogers, Farlan, Kilkenney, Drummond and I. And Rose.

The place was entered from a narrow alley off North Rampart Street. It was an upstairs room, huge and barnlike, without windows. What happened in the first ten minutes was exactly like any other Negro religio-sex orgy you might attend.

The room was dark except for a skylight through which some grey dimness filtered, and a large fire which had been built on a piece of sheet iron in the middle of the floor. We could see the wall for a little distance on each side of the fire. A mantelpiece-like board, more than head high, ran along it, and on this board sat a weird collection of gallon and two-gallon bottles, human skulls, goat skulls, dead chickens, and other things. Both ends of the room were in darkness, so that we had no way of knowing just how large the place was.

They were dancing when we entered, twelve couples in all, round and round the fire. It was a sensuous, writhing, lustful dance, and yet at no time did the men and women touch one another. Inside the circle, facing each other across the fire, stood a boy and girl. She was a beautiful child, not more than fifteen but already curving gracefully about the breasts and hips; a mulatto probably, and the firelight glowed richly on her skin. The boy was only a few years older, big shouldered, slim waisted, darker than the girl. They did not join in the dancing except for rare, sudden and uncontrollable movements. The only music was a weird sort of drumming which came from the darkness beyond the dancers.

After we'd watched about ten minutes, Rose McDonald leaned against me and whispered, "What are the boy and girl standing in the middle for? What are they going to do?"

"I don't know. Ask Kilkenny, he's probably seen these things before." She leaned past me and whispered to the big man on my left.

I TURNED to listen and was surprised by the look in his eyes. He was a handsome man with the lean, triangular face of a hero out of an adventure story—and he'd been the hero in more and wilder adventures than most persons ever read about. He was a man totally without fear; he'd been everywhere in the world, and not only that but he was a good engineer.

He was sitting the way mountaineers do sometimes, toes on the floor, buttocks resting on his heels. His shoulders were pushed forward, face set hard, eyes narrowed as he watched the dancers. I saw him glance toward the skylight, which showed the murky grey of October dusk.

Smiling, Rose whispered to him, "Why don't the men and women touch one another? I've seen more immorality at the Ralston Club with Gil Lombard playing."

Kilkenny whispered suddenly, "I think we better get out of

here." But even as he started to rise, he checked himself. It was already too late, though no one else realized the danger.

A woman was passing a bucket and cups around the circle of dancers. They drank thirstily, slushing the liquid over their chins. Another woman was offering a second bucket to the boy and girl in the center, and still a third was coming toward us. Already the music had picked up in tempo, become wilder and more eerie.

Kilkenny's whisper was fierce now. "Don't drink out of the bucket, but pretend to. Take a mouthful and hold it until she's gone."

The woman came down the line and we did as Kilkenny had said, though at the time I didn't know his reason. I was watching the dancers.

They were moving faster now, the men and women closer together but still not touching with so much as a finger. The movements of the dance, which had been no worse than those seen in a Harlem night club, were changing, taking on a hot, unleashed fury. Writhing, crouching opposite one another on the floor, wriggling upward, their faces growing wild, eyes rolling white in the firelight. And now and then, as they writhed close together, then apart without touching, I saw them look upward at the skylight with something in their faces that was almost madness.

The boy and girl in the center had begun to dance now, or perhaps it wasn't really dancing. They would move toward one another, the muscles of each twitching lustfully. And then they would stop. It wasn't the fire that stopped them. I don't believe they ever saw the big fire burning between them. It was as if some invisible wire held them apart despite their straining; and I saw them glancing madly at the skylight where only a dull gloom showed now.

The woman with the bucket had passed on. Kilkenny twisted and spit the fluid from his mouth. I did the same. "This is going to get hot," I whispered.

Kilkenny said, "Get the hell out of here, quick and quiet. You first, Archer."

Rose, who was close to me on the other side, heard him. She

said, "We can't go now. It's just getting good. What was in that bucket? It tasted funny."

"Get the hell out of here," Kilkenny said again. "I'll tell you about it outside." I could just see his face in the gloom. His mouth was like a straight scar and the firelight glittered in his eyes. All at once I knew that we were in danger.

I said, "Rose, we better get out." All of us were speaking in hushed whispers. The dancers themselves never made a sound except for their passion-filled breathing and the weird note of bare feet upon the boards. Out of the darkness to the left the drum sent its eerie, spine-rippling throb.

"I won't go," Rose said, and sat flat upon the floor. "I want to see what's going to happen." That was the way with her; she made up her mind and there was no changing it.

Kilkenny said fiercely, "Hell's going to pop in here. If we don't leave now, we may never leave." He moved close to Rose soundlessly. All the rest of us had turned and were watching him.

Rose said, "Don't you pick me up. I'll shout and get us all in trouble."

THERE was something in Kilkenny's face I had never seen before. I thought for a moment he was going to knock her unconscious and walk out with her. Then he glanced at the skylight.

"Listen," he said. "Those men and women won't touch one another as long as it's daylight, but it'll be dark in a minute. Then they're going crazy. They've been dancing all day without putting a hand on one another. And they've been drinking that stuff they brought us. It'll drive you sex crazy. I've seen it in Brazil. First it'll be the boy and the girl while they all watch. Then all of them. They'll be mad, I tell you. Your white skin won't save you. Those bucks'll kill us to get you. We've got to leave while we can!"

Rose stared at him and I could see how white her face had grown. She opened her mouth to speak.

The drums flared like exploding fire for one second, then dropped to a low-heard mutter. But that mutter was a sound so furious that it rippled through all the fibers of my body, hurting them. It was like the panting of an animal gone mad for sex. I looked toward the fire.

The women were passing the buckets again, and one was coming toward us, hardly visible in the gloom. The couples had stopped dancing. The men and women leaned toward one another fiercely, yet not touching. The boy and the girl in the center were half crouched, trembling. And all of them were staring at the wall beyond the fire. I could see the light gleam on the skulls and bottles that lined the high mantel.

I looked quickly at the skylight. The tiny pink flush was gone and there was only grey darkness.

"Come on," Kilkenny whispered. "Quick!"

We took one step, keeping close to the wall. Then the voice said, "Don't go, my friends. You have seen too much not to stay and join in the rest."

I think all of us turned in the same instant, like marionettes pulled by a single string. We were six men and Rose, but not one of us made a sound. In all that quivering darkness there was no noise except the drums, soft and furious.

The woman was beyond the fire, standing just under the high mantel which ran along the wall. She wore no clothes from the waist up and she was beautiful, more beautiful than I had believed it possible for a human being to be. Her skin was the color of the fire and smeared with some kind of oil that reflected the flames in weird and shadowed dancings. Her eyes were like flame too, and her mouth was like that of a vampire fresh with blood.

She said gently, "You shall stay and watch the rest of the ritual; you shall even take part in it. Perhaps then you won't be so anxious to destroy this building." The Negroes were moaning, making a sound like tortured spirits, begging her with a wordless whimpering to release the strange hold she had over them so that they might get at one another. And there were other bucks in the place now. I could see them to the left of the fire, and I could see the way their eyes blazed at Rose.

Kilkenny said, "I'm sorry. We have to leave." He jerked at my arm. "Get going with Rose, you fool!" His right hand was inside his coat, near the left shoulder.

I caught Rose by the hand, said "Came on," and stepped into

the darkness toward where I thought the door was. Two giant Negroes stripped to the waist rose like a wall in front of me. They had come out of nowhere, and now their eyes were on Rose, lust-filled.

Behind us the woman said, "You are going to stay." Then she said some words that I didn't understand—and hell burst in that room.

I heard a high, thin shriek and a sob and knew without looking that the boy and girl who had danced by the fire had clutched one another. The voices of the other dancers rose in a demoniac wail of passion. At the same instant the two giant bucks lunged for Rose.

I swung, and the sound of my fist striking was clear even under the storm of noise. But the giant didn't go down. Instead he swerved toward me. Rose screamed as the other Negro caught her.

It wasn't a clean thing I did, but it was the only possible one. My fists couldn't stop that giant. With all my strength I kicked him in the groin. He went down and I dived over him for the one who had Rose.

Behind me a pistol roared. There was the crashing of glass. I was struggling with the second negro now and somehow I got twisted so I was looking at the fire. Horror stabbed into me and for an age-long moment I was fixed like a fly stuck through with a pin, staring, unable to breathe or move.

The boy and the girl were writhing together on the floor, but I didn't notice them. The Negroes had gone mad. Some were charging toward us, screaming. Others had clutched one another and were oblivious to the noise of the shot or the screams. But I didn't notice them either and was not even aware at the moment of seeing them.

It was the woman at whom I stared.

CHAPTER TWO

RETURN FROM THE GRAVE

SHE STOOD with the firelight flickering over her oiled body. Her mouth, red as fresh smeared blood, was open in a snarl of combined hate and lust and agony. Her white teeth glittered and her eyes were slitted flame. Her high breasts stood straight and painfully beautiful from her body, catching the full glow of the fire. Just above the left one was a small hole. A thin stream of blood coiled down from it, straight for an inch or two, then curved to circle the breast. As I watched the blood began to move down across the flat and golden flesh of her stomach.

In the eternal second that I stood transfixed it seemed to me she was more desirable than a mortal woman could be, that she was lust incarnate drawing me toward her.

Then from her mouth came a cry that was not pain, but fury and something more than fury, a hatred beyond human feeling. "You shall not escape! Not one of you! From the grave I'll...."

Something struck my side, whirled me around. It was Kilkenny. Beyond him I saw McDonald and Kent Drummond trying to tear the big Negro away from Rose. "Get going, you fool!" Kilkenny shouted. He jumped and his gun swung up, then down. Rose staggered away from the falling Negro, I caught her, and we all went stumbling toward the door.

Feet pounded behind us. Kilkenny's gun boomed again, twice. Somehow we were reeling down steps, running along the alley, and the damp, semi-coolness of a New Orleans October night blew in our faces.

In my ears, sounding over and over, was the last thin shriek of the woman as it came from her twisted mouth: "You shall not escape! Not one of you! From the grave I'll...." I kept thinking of that last phrase: *from the grave.* What would she do from the grave? Fear put cold fingers around my heart.

BUT the next day the fear was gone. Mr. McDonald, Rose's father, and Mr. Rogers, the two oldest men of our party, were rather shaken up by the matter and by the brief police investigation that followed. Kilkenny merely explained that he had not intended to kill the woman but someone had jarred his arm as he fired. He had been trying to frighten off the attackers.

Bill Farlan laughed about it and said, "Well, boys, I got my story."

And Kent Drummond replied with bitter sarcasm, "Yes, and remember the several lives the story cost. But, of course, three or four human beings mean nothing to a good publicity man."

Drummond had never liked Bill Farlan. They were about as opposite as two persons can be. Drummond was young, thin, bitter; a brilliant chemical engineer and was interested only in his work and in socialism. He never seemed to find time to comb his hair or get his clothes pressed and he resented the expensive, too stylishly cut suits which Farlan wore over his plump figure. He resented me too, because I had been born with money. In fact, I think he hated everybody except Jock Kilkenny.

But the whole matter of *Varishti* passed and was forgotten. In January everybody went back to New York but me. Before Rose left she promised to marry me in February. Then I went over into the Cajan country in west Louisiana for a last bachelor hunt.

They don't have any newspapers in the swamp between New Iberia and Plaquemine and it was nearly a month before I got back to New Orleans. I'll never forget the feeling that came over me when I saw the newspaper story of Mr. Rogers' death. I stood there on Canal Street, dazed, reading the thing over.

The story was played up big because it had a local angle. Rogers and McDonald were both dead, killed the paper said, by some kind of curse which had been put on them in New Orleans. Both had died in exactly the same way, and horribly. McDonald had died first. Doctors had been unable to do anything for either of them, or even to guess at the cause of their deaths.

And all at once I was seeing that naked and beautiful body as it glowed in the firelight. And I was hearing the cry that held more than human fury: *You shall not escape! Not one of you! From the grave I'll....*

Abruptly I realized that I was muttering the words aloud. I dropped the paper and walked away, moving fast.

From the hotel I wired Rose, then arranged for a New York plane.

It was late twilight when the taxi put me out in front of the Riverside Drive apartment house where Rose lived. An icy wind whipped across the river, driving a thin spray of snow. I had only the clothes which I had worn up from New Orleans and I was freezing, but for some reason I stood on the sidewalk for a long moment looking up at the grey face of the building where lights were coming on in windows dimly seen through the snow.

Rose and all the others—all the others who were alive—were waiting for me in there. What would they tell me about the death of McDonald and of Rogers?

I plunged at the apartment house door, pushed it open and went in.

The elevator boy was not in the lobby, so I ran up the stairs without waiting. On the third floor I stepped into the hall and turned left. Rose's apartment was the second door down and I was half way to it before I noticed the man crouched there as though listening. But even as I noticed him he straightened and I saw he held a cigarette in one hand, a broken match stem in the other. He was a tall, gaunt man with a sharp-angled face that looked as if it had been cut from rust-colored iron.

"I beg your pardon," he said. "Have you got a match? I just broke the head off my last one and was looking for it."

"Sure."

"Thanks." He strolled toward the elevator. I rang the door bell.

ROSE answered and for a moment we stood looking at one another. I had never seen her so beautiful. She was wearing black and her face was paler than I had ever seen it. Framed by jet black hair she looked almost ghostly. "Darling," I said.

Then she was crying, her face buried against my shoulder while I held her. "Oh, I'm so glad you've come, Dave. So glad, so glad."

"I want to be with you, all my life, whenever you need me," I said.

After a few moments we went into the living room where the others were waiting. Kilkenny's handsome face was lined with worry. I knew that he had fought against the deaths of McDonald and Rogers harder than those two men had done, trying everything possible to save them.

Bill Farlan was on the sofa beside Kilkenny. His face was as round and pink as ever, his clothes as well cut and neatly pressed. But there was a change in him, something furtive and fearful back his eyes. He was afraid.

In a chair near the far wall, his mouth twisted as always in a thin, bitter smile, clothes wrinkled, hair uncombed, was Kent Drummond. He was the only one who did not speak when I came in.

We talked a few minutes about the work at the plant and about hunting in the Cajan country, but nobody really cared.

I said abruptly, "Tell me what's happened. All I saw was one story in the *Times Picayune.* They had a lot of stuff about curses and things."

Kilkenny glanced at Rose. She said, "Tell him, Jock. I don't mind."

"All right." He leaned forward, resting his elbows on his knees. "It started a little over two weeks ago. Mr. McDonald, Mr. Rogers, Drummond, Farlan and I were here talking over some work. McDonald went to light a cigar and found he couldn't feel anything with the tips of his fingers. While he was wondering about that he had an attack of some kind. It seemed to—well, drive him momentarily mad and to cause hallucinations. He got horribly frightened at Rogers and backed away from him, screaming. And then, out of sheer terror and desperation, he jumped at Rogers and would have killed him if we hadn't pulled him off. After he got over the attack he swore—" The puzzled look deepened in

Kilkenny's face and he swallowed—"he swore that he had seen the woman who cursed us in New Orleans, had seen her as she was when we went out, the blood running down over her breast. He had several attacks after that, each one preceded by a growth of the paralysis up his legs and arms. And every time he jumped on Rogers. Finally—McDonald died."

"And Rogers?"

"It was the same way, only he always jumped on me, thinking I was the woman. And the odd part of it is...." He paused. I saw him swallow again. "This sounds as if I'm making it up, but it's true. I had the damndest feeling each time, like I wasn't—wasn't myself. I'm not good at explaining things. I can't make you understand. But I couldn't raise a hand to keep him off me."

"What causes the trouble?" I asked. "What did the doctors say? What did they do?"

"The doctors," Kent Drummond said bitterly, "did exactly nothing."

"What about Dr. Layton Carman? He specializes in freak diseases, doesn't he?"

Farlan twisted nervously on his seat. "It wasn't a disease," he whispered, then shut his lips tight as though the words had slipped out.

Rose spoke for the first time. "Dr. Carman wouldn't come. You know he and Dad...."

I remembered, then. McDonald had interested the doctor in a business deal which had lost Carman a great deal of money. The former friends had become bitter enemies, Carman claiming he had been cheated.

KILKENNY had been holding a cigarette for a long time but he hadn't raised it to his lips. I happened to glance at it. The fire had burned down to where it was almost against his flesh. "He must feel the heat," I thought. But he paid no attention to it. The fire ate a little farther. It was to his fingertips now.

Suddenly I began to sweat.

I don't think anyone had been talking during the last few seconds, but all at once a new kind of silence came into the room.

It was a breath-taking silence in which I couldn't breathe and my lungs felt crushed against my ribs. Without moving my eyes from Kilkenny's hand I knew that all the others were watching it too.

Then Kilkenny began to lift the cigarette. He moved it with a tremendous, straining slowness. My gaze moved with it, up, up, until it was on a level with his eyes. The color of the smoke had changed because it was burning his flesh, but his fingers had never shifted.

Into that empty, aching silence he said, "I can't feel it. I can't feel it at all." His mouth stayed open after the words. His eyes were larger than I had ever seen them.

He got to his feet. He wasn't looking at the cigarette any longer. He was looking at me. His eyes were bulging and I could see the muscles in his neck pulled into cords. His lips were working, but he didn't say anything.

I was standing up, though I can't remember having moved. It was as if someone else had moved me, as though someone else had taken possession of my body and stood there watching the man across the room with my eyes.

"Go away," Kilkenny said. "Go away!" His voice was barely above a whisper, horrible. "I didn't mean to kill you. I was shooting to miss, to frighten you. Someone struck my arm." And then in a thin, piercing scream, "Go away!"

I never moved. I couldn't. I stood there, gaping.

Kilkenny went sideways along the sofa, then back to the wall. He moved the way an animal does, slinking, crouched. His face was grey with terror and he was slobbering. His hands were in front of him, one of them still holding the charred cigarette which had burned out between his fingers.

"Go away. Please. I didn't mean...." He was begging now, whimpering. He begun to crouch lower and lower against the wall until he was almost on his knees, groveling. "Please. Please...."

I took a step toward him. I don't know why I did. I couldn't help it. "Kilkenny," I said.

"Go away!" He was panting now, fiercely, horribly. The fury and terror of a cornered rat was in his face. And there was something else—lust. "Go away, for the love of God! I—" Then in sheer madness he drove at me.

I saw him coming. I seemed to watch him for a long time before he struck me. But I couldn't move. Someone else was inside my body and I might as well have been a third person to one side, watching. When he hit me I felt the pain, but I still couldn't resist. I went down and he fell on top of me, beating with both hands, tearing at my throat, using teeth and nails.

He kept screaming, "Go away! I didn't mean to kill you. I didn't mean to kill you!"

CHAPTER THREE

THE CURSE FALLS

SOMEHOW THEY got him off me. He fought for a moment against Drummond and Farlan, and though under normal conditions he could have handled them both, they got him to the sofa. I knew that fear in those few moments had drained his body more completely than a week's starvation would have done. Once on the sofa he relaxed, his head fell back, and he lay still.

Drummond said, "Well, he's fainted."

Rose was kneeling beside me before I saw her. "Oh Dave! Dave! Are you hurt badly?" There were tears in her eyes and she was touching my face with her handkerchief. When she took it away it was blood stained.

I said, "I'm not hurt, darling." I stood up, and helped her.

Drummond glanced toward us. "You can go wash your face," he said bitterly. "Kilkenny won't come to for half an hour and when he does he won't want to be reminded of where he hit you."

I went to the bath, moving stiffly. In a mirror I saw I had a slight cut below the left eye and the right corner of my mouth was bruised.

I bathed my face and put a touch of iodine on my cuts. My hands were fairly steady, but my heart beat was slow, too slow, and hard against my ribs. It took me a long time to get clean because I was remembering the inhuman and lustful beauty of a woman and I was remembering her cry: *You shall not escape! Not one of you!*

I shuddered. My hands were shaking when I put on my coat

and walked swiftly back to the living room.

Kilkenny was still unconscious. Drummond and Farlan stood at opposite ends of the couch. Rose ran to me and put both hands on my arm. "I'm afraid," she whispered. "That's just the way it was with Dad and Mr. Rogers. It's going to kill Jock too. I know it."

Farlan looked unnatural with his hair and clothes rumpled from struggling with Kilkenny. His lips worked dryly. "That woman said she'd get us all. Everyone of us. First it was Mr. McDonald and he thought Mr. Rogers was the woman. Then it was Mr. Rogers and he thought Kilkenny. And now Kilkenny and he thinks...."

Rose's short choked cry cut him off. I stood motionless, unable even to breathe; I knew what he meant.

Kilkenny had attacked me.

After he died, I would be next!

I felt hollow inside and cold. That was all at first. Then as the seconds dragged into eternity I hurt as though my heart had been jerked to one side. The muscles of my throat were swollen and ached, but still there was no fear.

All at once it came, storming up from my belly, howling like a great wind, battering at my brain, tearing it apart and I wanted to scream, run, fling myself blindly through the night.

Kent Drummond said, "Hell, a disease couldn't touch you. With all your money it wouldn't dare. Sickness is for the proletariat."

I beat down the fear, helped more by anger at Drummond than by my own courage. "To hell with you," I said. "I'll leave you my money and when you die a week later it'll break your heart because you haven't had a chance to be a capitalist very long."

"Dave! Dave!" Rose was shaking me by the arm. "We've got to do something. I can't lose you now, Dave. Dad's gone and.... You're all I've got now."

I put my arm around her. "It won't hurt me, sweet. We'll find out what it is and stop it." But deep inside my brain a voice was whispering:

You shall not escape! Not one of you! From the grave....

THIS took place on Tuesday. It was Thursday when the cab containing Kilkenny, Drummond, Farlan and I stopped in front of my apartment house. Stepping out into a cold, howling wind I shivered while I was paying the driver. Drummond got out and reached back to help Kilkenny. I was glad I didn't have to do it, because I didn't like to look at him now, remembering what he had been and how I admired him. His hands were paralyzed to the wrists, his feet to the ankles so that he walked with an odd, stiff movement.

But it wasn't that which I didn't like to notice. It was his face. Fear had eaten away the firm muscles and made them hang sloppily. His eyes held a hint of madness, big and dark against his grey cheeks. His mouth was always slightly open and drooling, so that he had to keep wiping the back of a stiff hand across it.

The driver handed me my change; I tipped him and turned toward the house. From the corner of my eye I saw a man round the corner and disappear. I had only a brief glimpse of his face and I couldn't be certain; yet he looked familiar. It was a rugged, sharp-cornered, brown face, as tough looking as if it had been cut from rust-colored iron.

Then I remembered. It was the man I had given a match outside Rose McDonald's apartment door. "I wonder why in hell I should remember his face," I said aloud, and went into the house.

In my apartment I poured four scotch and sodas. I tried to make my hand steady, my voice natural when I handed one to Kilkenny. But seeing the terror in his eyes, knowing I was marked for next, having no idea what I could do to protect myself; I was sick with dread.

"Dr. Carman will be here in a few minutes," I told them. "He'll fix you up, Kilkenny. He knows all the odd diseases in the world."

"It's not a disease." The words broke thin and sudden from Farlan's mouth.

Kilkenny swung at him insanely. "Stop saying that! Stop it, by God, or I'll...." His voice choked and he put his face in his hands. His paralyzed fingers were rigid across his forehead.

"And how did you get this angel of mercy to change his mind about McDonald's employees?" Drummond asked. "A rich man's power of persuasion, huh?"

"No. He says he thought it was some kind of publicity stunt at first."

"It was, at first," Drummond said. He looked at Farlan. "God! How I hate publicity men."

Kilkenny raised his face. The corners of his mouth were twitching but he was trying to hold them steady. "I'm sorry," he said. "I shouldn't have broken like that. I don't know what it is about this—this disease or curse—or whatever it is. I'm not afraid of dying. I've faced death before. But I can't face this. The fear's like a fever inside me. It rises up sometimes and there's nothing I can do about it."

"Hell," I said. "You're fighting it, and now Dr. Carman's coming to help. You'll get all right."

He looked at me and there was something in his eyes that made me shudder. He said, "No. I won't get all right. I'm going to die. It's not that I'm afraid of. It's the madness."

He stopped, and there was no sound in the room except the beat of wind against the windows. It seemed to whisper:

You shall not escape! Not one of you!

CHAPTER FOUR

MAN INTO MANIAC

A FEW MINUTES later Dr. Carman rang the bell and I let him in. I had never met him before that morning and I didn't like him, but he had a nation wide reputation. He had been sullen when I had approached him, refusing to come at first, saying that he hated McDonald even when he was in the grave, and hated everybody who worked for him. He seemed to feel that all McDonald's associates were equally guilty of his financial ruin. I had pointed out that he was a doctor and we needed him—and I had promised a fat fee.

He marched past me when I opened the door, big, square-faced, a white mane of hair over piercing eyes. "All right," he snapped, "which one of you is sick?" His eyes swept over us, stopped on Kilkenny. Without waiting for an answer he stepped toward him. "All right, tell me all you know about this."

"All right," Carman said when Kilkenny had finished. "Now let's look at you."

His examination was thorough. He stripped Kilkenny, stretched him on the sofa and went over him from end to end. "All right," he said when he had finished. I was getting damn tired of hearing him use that word. "Just where does this paralysis stop on you?"

"At the wrists. I can still bend my elbows without any trouble." He started to put his stiff right hand against his left wrist—and the whole arm moved! The elbow would not bend!

"Good God!" Kilkenny whispered. Terror came like a wild flame into his eyes. His mouth jerked open.

He tried to swing off the couch on which he was lying, but his legs kept straight, refusing to bend at the knees. "Damn it!" he said, "I've got to get up! Got to!" He began to struggle terribly, his stiff arms and legs thrashing.

I jumped toward him. "For God's sake, old fellow, steady. Stay there, we'll...."

Carman pushed me away. "I want to watch him," he said flatly.

Somehow Kilkenny got to his feet. His knees were slightly bent as they had been on the couch. His arms were bent at the elbows and he could neither straighten them nor bend them farther. He stood there, naked, stiff-legged, swaying from side to side.

And then he saw me.

The scream came horribly from his mouth. It ended in a gurgle and saliva spilled over his lips. His arms were held in front of him, the grotesquely bent elbows and the rigid fingers looking strange. There was insanity in his eyes, a mad, insane fear mingled with lust.

He began to whimper a prayer, the words drooling like the saliva from his mouth. But I was thinking about myself and the feeling that had come over me. I had the eerie sense of not being the person who stood there at all, of furnishing only the body from which another spirit watched and gloated in Kilkenny's madness.

"You can't come any nearer!" Kilkenny shouted. From a strange distance I heard his words. "You can't come nearer! I'll go mad! I'll go mad! Mad!"

His voice broke into a whining prayer, most of it unintelligible. I remembered having seen a madman once who always thought his guards were going to beat him and he crawled and whimpered. Kilkenny was that sort of man now. Terror had driven him insane.

Then all at once he was shrieking, high and furious. "You've got to go away! I killed you once. Now I'll...." He came at me, stiff legged, his arms rigid from biceps to finger tips, saliva drooling from his month. And my body stood there, unable to move, filled with this other spirit that I dared not guess at.

HE struck me, a wild blow swung from the shoulder, his arm stiff as a club. I staggered, but didn't fall. Then his lowered head caught me on the mouth. I went over backwards and he fell on me. With his arms stiff he couldn't hit me and he couldn't get up. He tried to bite my throat, slobbering like a mad dog. They pulled him off me, and while I still lay on the floor he fainted.

It was Farlan who picked me up. Instinctively I wiped my mouth and found there was blood on it. I went into the bathroom to wash.

Looking into the mirror while I washed my split lip, I noticed for the first time how much fear had already told on me. I had scarcely slept the last three nights and there were dark circles under my eyes. There was a muscle just above the split in my upper lip that jerked constantly. I could feel it, see it when I looked closely in the mirror. And there was something back of my eyes, a shadow that I dared not study.

In the living room I found Kilkenny still unconscious. Drummond had got a blanket and covered him. I asked Carman, "What is it, Doctor?"

There was a puzzled expression in his eyes, but they were still fierce. "I can't say definitely. It's a disease, of course." He paused, then said, almost harshly as though he were afraid of what we might answer, "You don't put any faith in that curse business?"

Nobody spoke, but I saw Farlan. He was saying silently, "It's not a disease. It's not a disease. I know."

"All right," Carman snapped. "Whatever it is, it seems to center on you fellows. It is probably contagious, but since all of you have been around the city and no one else has contracted it, I would say not highly so. But it is best that you be quarantined. You can go where you please to stay, your homes or wherever you want, but contact other persons as little as possible."

Drummond said, "I might as well hole up. Both McDonald and Rogers seem to have died broke. Now Kilkenny's off the job. With Archer pulling out I won't have any work anyway." He took a cigarette from his pocket, stuck it between his thin, bitter lips.

"I'll take charge of Mr. Kilkenny," Carman said. "Whatever this disease is, it affects the mind. Mr. Kilkenny has gone mad with fear. I have already called an ambulance for him. The rest of you will stay away from other persons!"

It was not three minutes later that the ambulance arrived. Carman had never taken off his overcoat and without a word of goodbye he stalked out after the men who carried Kilkenny.

Drummond, Farlan, and I looked at one another. I could feel the muscle jerking at the corner of my lips.

"Well," Farlan said at last. "What are we going to do?"

I didn't answer him. I couldn't. It's not a pleasant thing to watch another man, a brave man, go mad because of fear, to know that he is going to die horribly—and to know that you will soon be stricken by the same thing. It's not easy to wait for that sort of death, unable even to try to escape.

Drummond said, "I'm going to do what Dr. Carman advised. I'm going where I can be by myself and I'm going to stay there. What else is there to do?"

"I—I can't do that," Farlan stammered. "I'm—afraid."

"I'm not looking forward to it." Drummond turned his bitter dark gaze full on Farlan. "Damn you," he said softly. "Damn you."

"I didn't know!" Farlan whimpered. "I didn't know it would turn out this way. I thought we'd see the dancers and get the story and...."

Drummond said again, "Damn you."

I finally got the lump out of my throat so that I could speak. "I've got a place down in south Alabama," I said. "It was one of those Southern mansions before the Civil War. It's an old wreck now. We could go there. Nobody would be in twenty miles of us except a few Negroes to look after the house."

Drummond said, "No, thanks. We don't seem to have this but one at a time. Carman says it's contagious. If I've got it now, I've got it. If I haven't, well—I'll take my chances alone." He crossed the room, picked up his overcoat and hat, and walked out.

I looked at Farlan. He was jittery. His round face was white and his hair looked plastered to his skull. "What about you?" I asked.

He stared at me, his eyes getting large. When he spoke it was more to himself than to me, scarcely above a whisper. "It's not a disease. I know that. But McDonald jumped on Rogers, and Rogers had it. And Rogers jumped on Kilkenny, and Kilkenny had it. And Kilkenny jumped on you, and…." He turned suddenly, snatched his hat and coat from the chair where they lay, and bolted out the door.

I stood in the quiet room alone.

The wind beat against the windows. "You are next," it whispered. "You are next."

THE deep silence of the room crowded at my ears. When my heart beat I could feel it in my wrists and temples. The bivalvular beat said, "From the—grave. From the—grave. From the—" In that long eternity no horns sounded on the street below. No one passed along the hall outside my door. There was no sound anywhere, except the whispered beat of the wind and the throbbing of my heart.

Somehow I got courage to move, to break the horror that held me rooted in my tracks. I began to talk aloud, hoping the sound of my own voice would give me strength.

"Well, I can stay here or I can go down to that place in Alabama. I could be alone there and not trouble anybody. Here persons come in and out."

I thought of Rose McDonald. When I had left her in New Orleans we had planned to be married the middle of February. It seemed a thousand years ago, that parting in New Orleans. "Well, I'll never marry her now. This thing will probably get me in a few days, and I—" I choked, thinking of Kilkenny's face. If it had done that to a man as brave as he was, to me it would….

"At least Rose won't see me if I go south," I said aloud. "If Rose stays alone she'll be safe."

As I spoke I thought of the woman's voice saying, "You shall not escape! *Not one of you!*"

"Rose will escape!" I said fiercely. "If I'm not around, if there's nobody to give the disease to her, she'll get free." I kept saying that over and over until I convinced myself it was true.

Then, with my bags half packed and a south bound plane arranged for, I heard the hall door open. And when I turned around it was Rose.

Her mouth was firm, her little chin set hard. She looked at my bags, then at me. "You going somewhere?"

I said, "Away for a few days. Pittsburgh on business." I couldn't look at her. This was the last time I was ever going to be with her and I wanted to put my arms around her, hold her hard against me, cry and tell her that I loved her and would love her even when the madness was on me and I was dying.

She said, "I didn't know you had any business, much less in Pittsburgh."

"It's being on the verge of getting married that's made a business man of me. I've got to do something besides make love to my wife, so I thought I would get me a steel mill."

She said, "You are more on the verge of getting married than you know. You are going to get married tonight and I'm going to Pittsburgh with you."

She said the words flat and hard, the way you swing a stick. I felt as though I'd been hit in the chest. Even before I began to argue with her I was horribly afraid.

She stopped me. "There's no need of lying to me, Dave. I know that Dr. Carman told you to go into quarantine. And I know that you—" she bit her lips. "You think you're the next one to have this trouble. You are planning on going away alone, but you're not. I'm going with you."

"Who told you about the quarantine?"

"Dr. Carman telephoned."

I said, "That louse!" and began to walk up and down the floor. After a moment I stopped and faced her. "Listen. It won't do any good for you to come. If I've got it, I've got it and you can't help. You can only get yourself in trouble. If I haven't got it—why, I'll be back before long."

The wind beating at the windows kept whispering, "From the grave... From the grave...."

Rose said flatly, "You know it doesn't do any good to argue with me. I'm going with you."

CHAPTER FIVE

The House of Terror

IT DIDN'T do any good to argue with Rose. It never had. We got married in New Jersey that night and took the plane south. We sat beside one another, Rose's hand gripping mine, and stared out into the night. We didn't seem to be moving at all—only to hang there in the darkness, feeling the small vibration of the plane. Sometimes there were lights below us, twinkling for a few moments and then fading out.

"It's our honeymoon," Rose said, her hand tightening around mine.

"Yes." I swung half toward her, and checked myself. I wanted to put my arms around her, kiss her, hold her against me and make this the wedding night I'd dreamed about. But I was afraid to kiss her, afraid even of the touch of her hand. Suppose it were a disease and I already had it; then kissing her would....

She put her arms around me, pulled my head down against her breast. "Try to get some sleep," she said. "You've been up for days with Jock Kilkenny, doing all you could for him. And—" she hesitated, running her hand through my hair— "I know you've been worried. I know it's hard for you to just sit around and wait, thinking perhaps you'll be the next one. But nothing's going to happen now that we're away from the city."

I kept thinking, over and over, "Suppose I go mad and attack her. Nobody in the house but us. I might kill her! I might kill her!"

It was about noon the next day when the plane circled and came down on what passes for an airport outside Tuscaloosa. We took a taxi into the town, ate lunch, and I bought an automobile. By two o'clock we were on the Meridian Highway. "There aren't any white persons living on Myrtle Hill plantation anymore," I told Rose. "The Negro quarters are still about half full, or were the last time I was down hunting. There's a man named Bill Harris who lives in Sumpterville and who keeps an eye on the place for me. I wired him we were coming."

In Sumpterville I asked about Harris and found he was at Myrtle Hill. We drove on. It's a country of low, rolling grass-covered knolls. The narrow road winds white and dusty in the summer, but now it was muddy. Against the mud we had to go slowly, in low gear.

Dusk set in before we reached the place. It was one of those grey-blue winter twilights they have in Alabama, and that make you feel utterly alone and afraid even to speak aloud. The sky seems very close all around and when you see a pine tree, tall and slender and black against the twilight, it seems to join the sky and earth in a terrible, aching beauty.

And then, while the night hung poised above us, we rounded a curve in the road and saw the old house on top of the next hill, black and square against the sky.

Rose caught her breath sharply. "Is that it?"

"Yes. I wonder why there are no lights."

WE didn't speak any more. There was the sound of the motor laboring and of the wheels in the mud, but somehow they didn't break the eerie quietness of the twilight. On top of the hill the mud gave way to gravel as we turned into a U shaped drive. The house was in the center of the U and we stopped before the wide front steps.

I said, "Well, here we are." My voice sounded loud in the gloom and when I finished speaking silence clapped down like a glass bowl over us. Rose and I stood there looking at one another. Down the hill somewhere a whippoorwill called.

"How do you like the place?"

"I'd rather have come in the morning. It looks—strange this time of the day."

It was a big, unpainted house in which you could still see the ghost of classic beauty. One of the tall columns was gone, another pushed askew. The bannisters on the upstairs balcony were broken and an old hoe stuck crazily over what remained of the rail. Tall bushes pushed against the house from every side, reaching up to the high first floor windows. The whole house gave a single distinct impression, but at first I couldn't find words for it.

"The place must have been beautiful once," Rose said. She was whispering without realizing it.

"Yes. When the ladies used to come out with their hoop skirts. There were some very beautiful ladies here."

And then I knew what the house looked like. It was a woman who had been beautiful once, but now was old and ugly and insane; so insane she believed herself still beautiful; a mad old woman who cackled and flirted and wore the dirty clothes of a long forgotten period and great old fashioned earrings.

"I wonder where Harris is," I said. "And why don't we hear any noise from the Negro quarters?" But there was no sound, only that tense quietness into which the whippoorwill shrilled again.

"What kind of bird is that?" Rose asked. She was shivering as if from the cold.

"Just a whippoorwill."

I thought of what the Negroes called it: the bird of death.

Abruptly Rose whispered, "There's somebody in the house. I saw a light!"

"Hello!" I shouted. "Mr. Harris!"

A voice answered, muffled by the long hall. A white spot of light appeared far back and there was the clunk of shoes. Harris came out on the front porch, carrying a flashlight.

"Hello, Mr. Archer." He stood hesitatingly, not coming down to shake hands.

"You got my wire that I was coming with my wife? This is Mrs. Archer."

Harris bowed deeply. He was a man in his middle forties, tall, getting a slight pauch now.

"How long are you going to be here?" Harris asked. His voice sounded a bit frightened.

"About a month," Rose said.

Again the silence came down and we all stood looking at one another.

Harris began to speak, slowly. "I'm afraid you won't find it very good here, Mr. Archer. I couldn't get any niggers to come in and clean up the place for you. They all left the plantation this afternoon, every one of 'em. I fixed up the house as well as I could, alone."

The fear began to rise in my throat again. "What did the Negroes leave for? Haven't they been treated fairly enough?"

"It wasn't that," Harris said. He shifted the flashlight nervously from hand to hand.

"What was it?"

"I don't know exactly. Some kind of fool superstition. You know how niggers are. The rumor got around about some kind of African curse being on the place, a *Varishti* curse, whatever that is. It scared the niggers half to death. They cleaned out."

Rose gasped and swayed against me. I put my arm around her. In the grey dark of early night we stood there.

Finally I said, "Maybe they saw the newspaper stories about Mr. J.C. McDonald—he was Mrs. Archer's father—and the business I was connected with and that New Orleans curse that was supposed to be on us."

"I doubt it. It wasn't in the newspapers much around here. Maybe someone told old Uncle Bennie, the Voodoo doctor here, and Uncle Bennie spread the news. It may have been that way. But—niggers find out things funny."

Again the stillness came in, thick and terrible around us. And again the whippoorwill cried. Harris glanced toward the sound nervously. "The bird of death," I thought. Sweat was breaking out on my body although with the darkness cold had set in.

Rose said in that quick, decisive way of hers, "Well, we're going in and stay here. I can look after the house."

Harris let out a sharp breath, but the tenseness didn't leave him. "Yes, ma'am," he said. "I'll try to find you niggers tomorrow."

He led us back into the house, lighting lamps and showing us the rooms he had cleaned alone. But not once did he come closer than was necessary, and he made no move to bring our bags. A few minutes later he was gone....

A WEEK followed in which seemingly nothing of importance happened. Each day Rose would tell me, "See, there's nothing wrong."

Yet I knew that she was horribly afraid, and so was I. Without realizing it, I acquired the habit of constantly touching things with my fingertips. And each time my hand was stiff with fear and my heart cold.

"There'll be once when I see my fingers on something and can't feel it at all," I kept thinking. I tried to shut the thought out of my brain, and couldn't.

Harris had got servants, but after two days they left without warning. There had been others and they too had left.

I asked Harris to get us more. "I'll try," he said. "I had to go beyond Livingston for the last couple. Not many'll come."

"I don't care if you get them from Harlem," I said. "Just so we have somebody to cook and clean up."

"All right." He looked at me queerly.

A middle-aged Negro and his wife came out the next morning, saying that Harris had sent them. They always backed away from me when I went near them and they spoke in low, sullen voices. They added to the drawn feeling of terror that stretched through the house. Rose and I could hear them whispering together when we were out of the room, but when one of us approached they shut up instantly.

In the middle of the afternoon I left the house and went walking. It was a dull, cloudy day, cold for Sumpter County, and with a hint of rain in the air. The very bleakness of the day, the way the sky closed in over the low, rolling hills, seemed like a warning of some kind.

I went farther than I intended, turning homeward only when I knew there was no more than an hour of daylight. Because of the grey clouds it was already semi-dark.

Without warning, the man on horseback topped a low hill not fifty yards from me and stopped. For a few seconds the man and the horse were a bronze statue joining earth and sky. Then the man turned in the saddle and looked down at me.

I halted as though the blood had frozen in my arteries and a thousand internal spikes held me rigid. For even at that distance I knew the man, the sharply angled face as though cut from iron.

It was the fellow I had seen outside Rose's door, whom I had seen later outside my own apartment.

He did not notice me. He turned his horse's head, went over the brow of the hill and vanished.

I didn't move but stared at the place he had been. Who was he? The first time I had seen him had been only a few minutes before Kilkenny had his first attack. I had seen him again just before Kilkenny went mad. And now I saw him a third time.

That terrible feeling of impending doom rose furiously through me. Something always happened after this man's appearances. What was going to happen now?

Black fear smashed into me. With a howling cry I began to run. I had to get home! Had to, quick! If I could get to Rose, bury my face in her lap and hold her against me, nothing could happen. I couldn't go mad as Kilkenny had done if I had Rose's arms around me. The thought of what I might do to her didn't occur to me. I was afraid and I ran for her the way a child does for its mother.

I came at the house from the back, out of breath, reeling. On the steps I almost fell, but I got up them, pawed open the kitchen door and went in. A lamp was burning on the big table. Beyond it, half crouched, his eyes horror-white as he stared at me, was the Negro servant.

The sight of him made me furious for some reason, taking the fear momentarily from me. "Damn it," I said. "What's wrong with you? What the hell are you looking at?"

His thick, purplish lips moved but made no sound. His eyes rolled.

I struck the table so hard that some knives and forks on it jingled and the lamp quivered. "You're going to tell me what's wrong with everybody in this county!" I yelled. "Why do all the Negroes look at me like that?" I slammed my hand on the table again.

There was a change in the Negro's face. The pupils of his eyes had contracted so that it was hard to tell which way he was looking. I felt more than saw the direction of his gaze. I looked down at the hand with which I had beat the table.

I had driven the prong of a fork into the tip of my forefinger. The fork dangled when I raised my hand. *But I could not feel it!*

The Negro let out a long, mourning wail. Then he had passed me, bouncing against the far wall as he went. I heard his feet on the back porch, heard him fall heavily at the foot of the steps. There was the sound of him running, then silence.

I stared into the night after him. The fork still dangling from my finger.

CHAPTER SIX

The One Attacked Dies Next

IT SEEMED to me that I stood there through a crawling black eternity. My eyes moved slowly from the darkness which had swallowed the Negro to my fingertip where the fork hung swaying. I stared at it, feeling nothing.

I didn't know Rose was behind me until I heard her voice saying, "Darling, what's the trouble? You were shouting and then the Negro screamed. What happened?"

I didn't answer. I began to turn slowly, the fork rocking below my finger. And when I had turned so that she could see it, I raised my eyes.

The madness struck me like a blow.

It wasn't Rose who stood there! It was the mulatto who had died in New Orleans!

She was naked from the waist up, her skin oil covered; and though the lamplight had been steady enough a minute before it turned into a living, twisting thing when it touched her. It danced over her like light from an open fire, gold and flame colored, writhing over her naked body. Her hands were held out to me.

From the hole above her left breast the blood coiled downward, circling the breast and beginning to move in a thin red stream across her belly.

I was mad in the minutes that followed, mad with terror and with a blinding, inhuman storming of passion. Desire almost hurled me toward the woman and sickening fear snatched me back. She had to be dead with that bleeding bullet hole above her lung! I couldn't want her! Yet I was like a beast gone mad because of passion.

There was the sound of my own voice and I could feel my mouth open and jerking though I had no idea what I said. I only knew that she was coming toward me, with sinuously lustful movements. I didn't think of Jock Kilkenny insisting he had really seen her. I didn't think of the others at all. I was conscious only of the woman in front of me—and I knew that she was there, living with one blood-stained breast and a mouth red as fresh blood, though the New Orleans police had found and buried her months ago.

And I desired and feared her with an inhuman, tremendous passion.

She came toward me, her breasts swaying with the movement. I knew then that I was screaming though I couldn't recognize the words I said.

Something that was not courage and not altogether desire arose in me. It was insanity. There was no escaping and as a cornered rat turns to fight, so did I. But there was more than fear. There was lust like hot teeth tearing at my bowels.

I hurled myself at her, mouthing things that had no meaning. I struck her and we went down together, her face close under me, my fingers warm in the blood and flesh of her breast. I shrieked and beat at her face.

Gradually the blackness covered my brain.

CONSCIOUSNESS returned slowly. I knew that I was lying down but I couldn't see anything. For a few horrible, confused moments I couldn't remember what had happened though I was still afraid. Perhaps you will understand the feeling if you have been very sick with a high fever that gave you nightmares and made you rant and you remember how later you lay in the bed, the fever still hot inside you, and you were unable to recall your dreams though you were still afraid of them. I felt that way, lying there with my eyes still shut. But the dreamer knows he shall eventually awake and be well—and I *knew,* even before I could remember distinctly, that it was *real.* Whatever the horror, it actually existed and I was afraid to open my eyes.

A voice said, "Darling, are you feeling better now?"

Memory came to me then, sickening and furious. I put my arms around Rose and pulled her down to me, still afraid to open my eyes. I remembered the woman, remembered attacking her with blind, animal lust and fury. "But it really was the woman," I told myself. "I know that. Kilkenny thought I was the woman and he jumped on me. But I k*now!* I'm glad that she was really there and I struck her, because otherwise...."

My eyes opened and I looked at Rose. I wanted to scream, to howl, to tear at my own eyes and throat and rip out the terror inside me. For though Rose had washed and powdered carefully I could see bruises on her cheeks and forehead, and there was a cut at the left corner of her mouth!

"Are you feeling better, darling?" she asked. Then she saw the fury in my eyes and said quickly, "You're all right, Dave. There's no one to hurt you. Be quiet."

"But she was here!" I said fiercely. I knew I had seen her, had struck her. There was no possible doubting it.

Rose said, "Be quiet, darling. As soon as you are a little better I'll drive to Sumpterville for a doctor."

I sat up, pushing her away from me. "I don't need any doctor. I don't want one. It's that woman. We've got to get away from her. She's here. I saw her."

Rose said, "Be quiet, darling. It's quite all right now."

But I saw the look in her eyes. I caught her by the shoulders and shook her. "The woman was here. I fought her. I didn't mistake anybody for her—did I?"

I knew before Rose nodded what her answer would be. I had known all along and I was sick at the stomach.

McDonald had attacked Rogers. Rogers had fought Kilkenny. Kilkenny had fought me. And now I....

I would die horribly as the others had done—*and Rose would be the next!*

I began to whimper, to claw at the sofa, to bite the dead ends of my fingers, beat them viciously against anything in an effort to feel. I was whining, insane with terror, and all the time I was ashamed of my fear. I wanted to be brave and couldn't. It's impossible to explain the feeling, but it existed. I saw myself like another person, cringing and mad with dread.

After awhile I got better control of myself. I stood up. "Listen," I said. "You're not going after any doctor. We've had the best doctors in the world and they've done no good. The reason is they—they thought Kilkenny and Rogers and your father were wrong. They weren't."

"What do you mean?" Rose asked. There had been fear in her eyes all along, but it was changing now. She thought I was insane.

I said, "This sounds crazy to you, but it's not. I can't explain, but that woman was in the kitchen with me awhile ago. The doctors can't help. You know they can't. We've got to get away from the woman. We've got to hide."

Rose put her hands on mine. Even then I thought how beautiful she was, her pale face framed in black hair. "The woman's dead," Rose said. "She couldn't have been here, unless...."

She was thinking, even as I was, hearing inside her brain the thin shriek: Not one of you shall escape! *From the grave.*

SOMEHOW I choked down the fear that shook me. I said, "Perhaps she's not really dead. Perhaps she escaped." I knew I was wrong, but I was trying to give Rose something to believe in. "Or perhaps she's really dead," I went on. "Strange things have happened before that nobody could explain. Anyway, she was here and we've got to get away from her. We'll hide."

I leaned forward and put my mouth so close to Rose's ear that nobody, no matter how near they were standing, invisible or otherwise, could hear.

"We'll go to a fishing camp I have," I whispered. "It's far back in the swamps. Nobody could ever find us there. Nothing—*human* could find us."

Rose grew taut, then relaxed. For a long minute she stood looking at me. I knew her thoughts as well as if she had spoken them. She thought, "He's insane. He's insane like the others. Or perhaps he isn't insane. Perhaps none of them were. The doctors can't help. Perhaps he's right and this is something beyond human understanding and our only chance is to hide."

Then suddenly her whole body was rigid and I knew she was thinking, "If it's not human, how can we hide from it?"

I knew she was thinking that. I had been thinking about it myself. I said, "It's our only chance. We don't understand it. We may be able to hide from it. It's our only chance."

"All right," she said. "We'll go."

I said, "Get some food together. I'll pack some clothes."

Ten minutes later I was back downstairs with two small bags. "Are you ready?" I called.

While I waited for Rose's answer there came the sound of a car on the gravel drive. Then shoes pounded the front steps, crossed the porch. A heavy fist knocked at the door. I put down the bags and went to it, slowly. When I opened it the yellow lamp light spilled out into darkness. Dr. Layton Carman stood on the sill, his white hair brushed back in a fierce mane, his dark eyes glowing.

"Hello," he said, and thrust out his hand.

I didn't touch it. "What are you doing here?"

The question seemed to embarrass him and for the first time he appeared a human being with emotions. "All right, I don't blame you for not liking me," he said. "I was an ass in the early part of this disease. I let your father-in-law die without trying to help him. But I want to make up for that. I want to help you and your wife. That's why I followed you here."

"Did you help Kilkenny?"

He flushed and it looked strange against his white hair. "No. Mr. Kilkenny died." Then he added, "But I've been learning. I know more now."

I started to tell him to get the hell out, that I had no use for him or any other doctor. But just then Rose came in. It was she who made the final decision.

"We'll stay," she told me. "We'll give the doctor a chance. He knows more about weird diseases than anybody anywhere."

I said, "It's not a disease." Only dimly was I conscious of having heard Bill Farlan say those words.

There's no need of describing the night and the day that followed. I lived through them feeling always the dark shadow of something hovering over me, something that I could not escape. I felt shut in, hopeless, the way a fox must feel when cornered by hounds. I waited for the thing to come again, knowing I couldn't avoid it.

And at twilight the next day, despite the medicines Dr. Carman had given me, the woman came. The attack was similar to that of the night before, but more hideous and frightful. I found suddenly that my hands were stiff to the wrists, my feet to the ankles, so that I swayed when I walked. And then I saw the woman exactly as I had the night before. She came at me, caught me in her arms and passion and fear ripped into my brain until I felt the fibres crack like threads of a spiderweb. And finally I fainted....

Carman told me, after I regained consciousness, that I tried to kill Rose but he had pulled me away before I hurt her badly. Then he went out and left me in the lamplighted room alone.

I can't explain the terror that was in me. I was cold all the way through and my brain hurt because of the fear pressing against it. The corner of my mouth jerked constantly, my eyes bulged searching the darkness. There's no doubt that I was partially mad, that inside the circling fury of my terror, my mind worked with the intense sharpness that marks the thinking of the insane.

"I've got to get away," I thought. "I can't stay here any longer. She'll kill me the next time she comes. I can't stay here and wait for her! I can't! I've got to hide."

When I stood up quietly I was thinking of Rose only as someone who might try to stop me. Whether I would harm or help her by running away I didn't consider. Nothing was in my mind then but fear of the *Varishti* woman and desire to escape from the place where she had found me.

CHAPTER SEVEN

FLIGHT FROM HELL

I OPENED THE front door quietly and went out. It was difficult to walk down the steps because my ankles would not bend, but I made it. Night had come, dark and moonless. I could barely see the line of the drive against the tangled horror of what had once been a formal rose garden, but was now a wilderness of weed and briar. I did not choose a direction consciously. I was spurred only by the desire to escape. My shoes made an eerie sound on the gravel, striking flatfooted each time because my ankles wouldn't bend.

Once I looked back to see the house black and gruesome against the sky. "It's like an old woman," I said aloud. "A mad old woman who thinks she's still beautiful." And at the same time I thought of the mulatto with her swaying, bloody breast and her arms out toward me. I began to run, blindly, insanely, falling time and again, fighting erect despite stiff hands and ankles, sobbing. And always running, running until my lungs were filled with fire and my mouth was open, cottony, my brain bursting; running still, trying to shriek out the fear inside me but unable even to sob now, my throat as though a white-hot iron had been thrust down it, but going on, madly. And then my ankle struck something and I fell down and lay in darkness.

When my lungs were working normally and my muscles would hold me, I stumbled erect and began to run again. I still had no sense of direction. It was only the fear behind me that beat me on. Terror had blinded me more completely than the night. I kept running.

Later I began to reel. Inside the fury of my insane brain I knew it was impossible to hold out much longer. And when I realized that, the fear became stronger than ever. "I've got to keep running," I thought. "If I stop, she'll find me. I've got to keep running forever."

I don't remember falling and I don't remember losing consciousness.

It was daylight when I looked about me again, a grim, ugly winter dawn. I was in the middle of a swamp with tall cyprus and water oak shutting me in on every side. A thin sheet of water covered most of the ground but there were occasional hillocks of yellow mud and tufts of dead grass. I was soaking wet, and cold.

Memory struck clean and vicious into my brain. I was afraid, as afraid as I had been the night before. The muscle at the corner of my mouth was twitching and when I held out my rigid hands the whole arms, from elbows down, shook. But some of the madness had gone out of me and I could think a bit more clearly.

The only swamp I knew about was near my fishing camp. In which direction, I had no idea, but I started. I had to keep moving because of the fear and because of the cold too. And despite the terror inside me, I was hungry.

It was late afternoon before I found a place I recognized and almost dark when I reached the fishing cabin. There was dry wood, fishing tackle, matches, a stove, and a few cans of food. "We brought those cans here a year ago," I thought. "But if they are no good I'd rather die of ptomaine poison than the way I'm going to die."

I kept my back turned to the door, kept refusing to notice the thickening darkness. Every attack Kilkenny or I had suffered had come just after dusk—at the exact time the *Varishti* dance had turned itself into a murderous hell. "I won't think about it," I told myself. "I won't think about it getting dark."

But I couldn't keep from thinking. Fear ached in my heart and lungs.

It was damned hard to get a fire started. I took some of the fat kindling wood and rested it on top of the stove. Finally, holding a match between both stiff hands, I managed to strike it and get the wood burning, then shove it into the stove. Once my right hand got too close to the flame. I saw the blaze curl around a fingertip and there was the smell of flesh, but no pain.

The woman didn't come that night, though I sat hunched in the gloom of the cabin waiting. An hour after complete darkness I knew she wasn't coming. "I've lost her," I tried to tell myself. "She can't find me here. I'll get well. I'll get well."

And then I began to think about Rose.

Suppose I did get well hidden here in the swamp? What would happen to Rose? It might be that the woman was driving her mad even now. Tonight, perhaps, the woman had come to her, paralyzing her body, sending fear to rip her brain apart.

"But Rose won't be hurt," I told myself. "It never comes to one until the other is dead. Rose won't be hurt until I'm dead. If I can save myself, I'll save her." I said that over and over again, but the dread stayed with me. Perhaps I made myself believe it a little—perhaps it was only the fear of what would happen to me that kept me from going back. Anyway, I stayed at the cabin.

AND though for two days nothing happened, I couldn't shake myself free of the horror. I lived in that cabin with fear like a roommate constantly at my side. When I went fishing in order to eat, terror went with me. When I crouched in the dark, listening to the night sounds in the swamp, terror crouched across from me and I was conscious of its presence. I did not sleep though now and then, from sheer exhaustion, I fell into a sort of drugged stupor. The corner of my mouth jerked constantly and saliva was always nasty over my chin. My eyes ached from their nervous shifting, searching for the body of terror in every shadow.

And then, an hour before dark on my third day in the swamp, I saw him! It happened without warning. I was a half mile from the cabin, pushing through a screen of muscadine vines when I looked up and there he was, not five yards away. The man with the face like rust-colored iron!

It sounds odd to say that the sight of a rather normal looking human being made a maniac of me. But I knew in the instant I saw him that the final night of horror had come. Three times I had seen him, and each time the *Varishti* woman had followed on his heels. Now I knew that she would come again tonight. And insane terror ripped at my brain.

I yelled, hoarsely, and began to run.

I didn't look back, but I heard him behind me, heard his breathing, the sound of his feet and the way he crashed through the brush. My ankles were as stiff as they had been but I had learned to move with a high swinging lift of the knee and I made good time.

"If he touches me," I thought, "my brain will burst like a glass shell. I'll go altogether mad, mad with fear. Even death won't stop my fear if he touches me." And I ran, making no sound except for my breathing and the noise I made in running. He never cried out, though I could hear him behind me and knew that he was gaining.

I crossed the small creek once, diving, swimming hard, clawing out on the far side. He came after me without hesitating, wrapped in that weird silence. I cut deeper into the swamp. The mud sucked at my stiff feet and he gained. I swung back toward the stream.

I didn't feel the effects of physical exhaustion until they struck me suddenly.

One instant I was running hard, and the next I could run no longer. My lungs were fire and my muscles water. I sprawled headlong.

THERE were not more than five minutes of daylight left. In the thick wintergloom of the swamp I stood and looked at the cabin. The door was yellow with light and I knew the lamp inside was burning. Someone was there.

I wanted to pray to find some relief for the terror gnawing at my belly, but I could make no sound. I wanted to turn and go plunging madly into the swamp, and I couldn't. "If I could only die and get relief from this torture," I thought. "If I could die and know that I would never hurt Rose!" But I was not going to die, not yet. There was no escaping what had to come. Bending my knees to swing stiff ankles, my hands rigid at my sides, I went forward.

I stepped through the open door of the cabin, and stopped.

Rose was on the far side of the room. I saw her turn, saw the pale beauty of her face in the lamplight, the dark hair, the hands outstretched. "Dave!" she cried, and then she had crossed the room and had her arms around me, her body pulled hard against mine. I tried not to think of her, not to notice the feel of her body. There were only a few minutes now and the *Varishti* woman would come. When she did, I would try to kill Rose, try to tear her throat apart with my hands.

"Dave!" Rose sobbed. "Oh darling, we've been looking for you everywhere. Bill's here, Bill Farlan. He can save you!" She turned, keeping her right arm around me, and pointed at Farlan, who stood near the lamp. "He's found out what's causing all this. He can save you."

"All right," I said. I was panting heavily. Nothing could save me. The *Varishti* woman was coming. It was not more than two or three minutes now.

"It's not supernatural," Farlan said. "It's the work of that damned socialist, Kent Drummond. I can stop him, but he's got a big organization. It'll take money, cash money and a lot of it, and I'll have to work fast."

"I've got the money," I could scarcely talk now. "You can have it, everything. But hurry! Hurry!"

"Okay," Farlan said. "Can you write me a check, to cash, now?"

Rose said. "I knew he needed money, so I brought some checks and a pen."

Farlan helped me to the table. Rose closed my fingers around the pen and I wrote. It was a bad signature, but it would do. I straightened and tried to step back from the table.

My foot scraped along the floor because the knee had not bent. My right arm, crooked at the elbow to write, stayed that way!

Rose screamed hoarsely, "Oh darling! You can't let it get you! Not now!" She ran to me.

And then I saw the woman!

The lamplight wavered like golden flame over her oiled body. Her flesh and shape had never been as hideously beautiful as at that moment. Above the perfect shoulders the lascivious and agonized face snarled in hatred and desire. The blood still coiled from the wound over the left breast.

I remember that I made an effort to stay sane, a furious effort like a man clawing at the edge of a cliff as he slips over. I remember thinking I heard the sound of my brain snapping like wires pulled too tight. And after that I remember nothing but the wild terror that engulfed me.

The woman's face was close. I caught it, sank my fingers into throbbing flesh. There was the sound of screaming, but who made it I didn't know. I was insane and I fought as a madman does. I knew I couldn't win but perhaps I could kill the thing under me.

There was one sharp flash of sanity. I thought of Rose. I thought, "Oh, God! I've killed my wife!" After that came a long, long period of darkness.

THAT was in February. It's May now. From my apartment window I can look across to Central Park and see the green hill tilting upward to a sharp rock ledge, see the trees in the breathtaking green of early spring. Even the children playing on the grass stop now and then without knowing why, amazed by the odor of growing things and the warm sun. Nurses are pushing innumerable baby carriages along the Fifth Avenue sidewalk.

I look back down at the paper on which I have been writing. I've finished the story now. I feel a little amazed that I am alive to finish it, that I can even explain it. But I owe my life to another man, a plain, hard-boiled, New York City detective with a face that looks as if it had been made from rust-colored iron. He had been assigned to the job after Mr. Rogers' death and had stuck to the end.

It seems that after the *Varishti* affair in New Orleans, Bill Farlan got an idea. He'd spent some time in Africa as the publicity man for an expedition and had learned of a little known disease which the natives called B'walla. It was a kind of tropical fever which caused temporary paralysis of the hands and feet. And it also caused hallucinations, just as almost any high fever will do. The natives don't mind the disease because it is never fatal and they have learned that the hallucinations, which are particularly vivid with this disease, concern the thing the victim is thinking about at the time the attacks come—and they always come around twilight, which is the time almost any fever reaches its height. Farlan had learned that the disease is the result of being mildly poisoned by a certain kind of berry. Dr. Carman finally recognized the disease in me and was able to furnish most of this information.

Knowing all this, it was easy enough for Farlan to give the disease to McDonald and to be present the first twilight that it took effect and make certain that McDonald was thinking of the *Varishti* woman. He had also managed to slip a drug into McDonald's food which has a terrific effect on the pituitary gland with the result of causing excessive fear. Prize fighters use the kidney punch because, they say, it saps the opponent's courage. This drug was similar in effect but a thousand times magnified.

Eaten by this drug and suffering from the African disease which the doctors were unable to diagnose because of its extreme rarity, McDonald came to the verge of insanity. Then Farlan went to him, explained that he had learned the cause of the disease and could cure him but it would take a large sum of money and McDonald would have to keep absolutely quiet about it. He got the money, fed McDonald the berry, which caused the disease in such excessive amounts that it killed him. He was repeating the performance with each one of us who had money.

The detective, Dr. Carman and Bill Farlan all followed me to Alabama without any of them knowing about the other. But there the detective learned about Farlan. He already had an idea of his guilt. He ran me down in the swamp that day, told me that Farlan had brought Rose to my cabin. Farlan had found me the day before and added more of the berry to my food in order to cause an attack the next night. He meant for me to kill Rose; then he would have poisoned me so that I died. No one would ever have known that he even had been in Alabama. The detective wanted me to go ahead, play with Farlan so that he could get the last evidence needed, with Rose for witness.

And the odd part of it is, thinking so hard about Farlan that last night, I fought and almost killed him instead of Rose. Farlan admitted he had used hypnotism to direct the attacks always at the same person. He was a pretty fair hypnotist, and since his victim was both sick and doped, it made the thing easy.

I'll get well, probably. Rose says I'm already well. But I'm still afraid when night comes darkling and a cold wind blows out of the twilight. Something wrenches at my heart and before me there is the vision of firelight on a naked body, of blood coiling about a perfect breast.

THE END

WYATT BLASSINGAME

DEATH UNDERGROUND

Deep within that stygian shaft lurked a monstrous living something which brought burning agony and slow, inevitable death to those foolhardy ones who went below. A blood-chilling tale of tingling terror and dark conflict underground!

KEN MARLOWE stared across his desk top, littered with blue prints and yellow sheets of paper, at Earle Brady, vice-president of U.S. Mines. Short, compact, with a square, determined chin and hard gray eyes, Brady glared back at him, hit his chair arm softly with his open palm.

"By God! That's every cent U.S. Mines will offer. You can take it or leave it!" Brady's short, big-knuckled fingers crushed a yellow sheet of paper.

At the end of the table Frank Crim, Marlowe's partner and half-owner of Southern Coal, said quietly, "That settles the matter, then. We won't sell."

Both Marlowe and Brady swung in their chairs to face Crim. The shadow of a question flickered in Marlowe's brown eyes. "The offer sounds fair to me, Frank."

Brady flung around in his chair, his shoulders hunched across the desk toward Ken Marlowe. His short fingers opened suddenly, viciously, and the crumpled paper rolled across the desk. For a moment Brady watched the man across from him.

Ken Marlowe was a pleasant-looking man; lean, brown, with light brown hair and wide shoulders that opened like a trumpet from narrow hips. His level eyes held Brady's intense gaze.

"I hope you can make your partner see what's good for him," Brady snapped. "I'm leaving for Pittsburgh tomorrow afternoon. I'll be out of here in the morning. If Mr. Crim has come to his senses—" Brady looked toward Crim sitting quietly at one end of the desk, nodded curtly— "well and good. If he hasn't—I'm leaving for Pitt, anyway."

Brady pushed back his chair, stood up. Marlowe and Crim got slowly to their feet. Crim was a short man but heavy shouldered. His face was round and peaceful, but there was determination and will in the hard lines of his mouth and the glint of his blue eyes. "We'll be glad to have you out, but—" His voice broke abruptly.

THE door behind him burst open. A lean man in grimy overalls leaped into the office. His mouth was open and his chin worked vigorously, but for a moment he was too winded to speak. Coal-dust had blackened almost his entire face, accentuating the whites of his fear-widened eyes. "Mr. Marlowe!" he gasped. "Mr. Crim, there—there's somethin' in that—mine!"

Marlowe jerked to his feet and swung toward the man, moving like a boxer, on the balls of his feet. "What the hell are you talking about, Wilson?"

"There's somethin' in that mine!" the foreman said again.

He was catching his breath now and his words, in a torrent of fear, seemed to pour over one another. "They been hearing it before, down that abandoned shaft. It's had the Negroes scared for two or three days, 'cept nobody could be certain they'd really heard it before today. I figured they was scared, 'cause a fortune teller told a couple of 'em this was a haunted mine. But a little while ago we all heard it.

"One of the Negroes, Ed Reilly, went to see what 'twas. Nobody'd go with him and nobody heard nothin' from him for a long while. Some more was 'bout to go look for him when—when he yelled—" The man repressed a shudder. "He yelled like old Sam Mason did when that tram car smashed his leg and he lay there across the tracks, yelling, 'fore anybody could get to him.

That's the way Ed yelled. We all knew it was Ed. Then his screamin' stopped. Not all at once; it slobbered off, kind of, gettin' deeper and lower like—like he was bein' dragged off—deeper into the shaft."

The foreman's voice slid to a stop and his frightened eyes, white and wide in his coal-blackened face, shifted rapidly on the three men, then back to Marlowe. The little office was very still.

Marlowe snapped, "Where is the man Ed Reilly? What's happened to him?"

Wilson's eyes shifted nervously. "He—he's still down there, I reckon. There ain't nobody else down there. All the men come flyin' out. I come out to tell you. I reckon that Ed—" His voice trailed off.

Marlowe spun on his heel, took one stride back to his desk, jerked open a drawer. Snatching up a flashlight and an automatic, he thrust the gun in his right coat pocket and spun toward Wilson. "How far'd he go down that shaft?"

"That shaft ain't very long," Wilson said slowly, "four-five hundred feet, maybe. We was right near the mouth. He musta gone pretty near the end, 'bout where it runs into the underground creek."

"All right," Marlowe said, his lips pulled thin. "I know where the shaft is." He swung past Wilson, went out the door.

Miners filled the little yard around the office, huddled in groups about the mine mouth, though Marlowe noticed that none of the groups were very close to the round, gaping hole in the hillside. Warm sunshine glinted on the coal dust that lay thick on the ground, gleamed on sweaty faces, brought into contrast the wide, rolling eyes of the Negroes.

As soon as Marlowe stepped out the office door a dead silence spread over the groups. They stood without moving, hardly breathing, as they watched Marlowe cross the narrow strip to the mine's mouth, plunge inside.

THE shaft ran into the hillside almost parallel, slanting downward gradually: a little tram line, over which the cars of coal were hauled, lay down the middle of the tunnel. As Marlowe swung inside, the tunnel seemed to smack its lips, then darkness swallowed him. He snapped on his flash.

The white spray of light that gleamed on the steel rails, showed the small cross ties blackened with coal dust. The walls of the tunnel pressed closely around him, seemed to push near and nearer as he went deeper. The darkness seemed tangible, intense, pressing closely about him. He could hear his soft crunching footfalls in the thick coal dust, a sound that seemed to weave and quiver in the dank, unmoving air.

Marlowe felt a strange, unreasoning fear clutch at his lungs; the fear of nameless things that comes to many persons underground or shut in by narrow walls. He shook his head. "Claustrophobia," he thought. "I always did hate to go underground."

But there was more than claustrophobia to fear here, under millions of tons of rock and coal and earth. Something had happened to a man here, something strange, unexplained had tortured, perhaps killed him. What had caused the man to scream horribly—and equally horribly, to cease screaming? An animal, perhaps? But what sort of beast would make its lair hundreds of feet underground?

He flung the light along the wall to his right. Twenty feet ahead a deeper blackness clung to the wall. The mouth of the abandoned shaft. His right hand went to his coat pocket, came out clutching the automatic.

At the entrance to the unused shaft Marlowe paused, flicked the light down the tunnel. In the intense darkness the white beam seemed to travel interminably through empty space. There was no track in this shaft, which slanted down at a sharper angle than the other. The floor was rough, uneven but so filled with coal dust that the rough spots threw no shadows, and the ground looked smooth and oily.

Beyond the light, darkness crouched like a black beast about to spring.

Marlowe turned into the shaft, went down it. Abruptly he halted. His heart stopped for a moment, then pounded against his ribs. From somewhere ahead had come a sound, a low rippling noise without form, whispering into silence. Marlowe's ears strained, the tiny muscles back of his ears grew taut.

He drew a deep lungful of dank air, released it slowly. "Damn it," he said aloud. "I'm getting jumpy as Wilson. Nerves, I suppose. And over nothing. I forgot there's a creek up here, with water rippling in it."

A flat echo beat back against his ears. He had not realized that he had been whispering until the echo had come to him. Through thin lips he laughed hoarsely, without humor. Flicking the light ahead of him from wall to wall, he went forward.

This was where the tunnel ended, on the side of an underground stream. To the right and left of the tunnel, Marlowe knew, ledges lay alongside the stream. The Negro must be on one of those ledges. And along that ledge, too, must be the thing that had made him shriek in agony.

Marlowe's fingers went hard around the butt of the automatic. Whatever it was, he'd find out in the next five seconds.

His light glinted on the slick, oily waters of the creek, along what he could see of the ledge, eyes straining at the darkness. Then he stepped out of the tunnel's mouth onto the edge of the creek.

Marlowe's light swept to the right, stopped. The muscles along his jaw jerking, his heart feeling swollen and still, Marlowe staggered backward as though sheer horror had struck its hairy paw against his chest.

THE white spray of light showed the body of Reilly lying naked, horribly contorted and grotesque beside the edge of the stream. The body was wet, glistening, and water had darkened the ledge under it.

Then, as Marlowe staggered back, something slimy and snake-like struck at his face from the darkness. Marlowe felt it strike his temple, slither across his cheek. Cold, creeping chills tingled from his face to his spine, and down his back. Jerking up ins gun, he spun on his heel, sent the shaft of light searching the darkness.

Abruptly the light stopped. Every muscle in Marlowe's body taut, he stared at the cloud of smoke that completely hid one end of the low, vault-like space beside the stream. It was a heavy, impenetrable murk. And through the dead, unmoving air it writhed slowly upward into darkness. Marlowe flicked his light to the low ceiling and watched the smoke bank against it crawl along the coal like a live thing.

The air tore from Marlowe's lungs in a gasp of agony. The right side of his face where the formless, snake-like thing had struck seemed to burst into flames! Hot pain ripped his cheek and forehead.

Instinctively he jerked up his right hand, holding the gun, and rubbed his knuckles across his face. The barrel of the automatic scraped his forehead as he struck frantically at his cheek. His breath wheezed through his nostrils in agonized gasps.

Fighting the pain that flamed in his face, the terror that clutched like a skeleton hand at his heart and lungs, Marlowe held the gun ready and stepped to the edge of the swirling smoke. The flash, held close to the smoke, jabbed faintly through it. Marlowe swept it across the ground, then up. He stepped into the smoke, moved forward three slow steps. The vapor stung his eyes and nostrils; he held his breath and went on. The light glinted on something black, unmoving. Breath hissed from Marlowe's lungs. He had reached the end of the vault—and had found the dead body of Reilly, the smoke, and the horror of the slithering monster. And—firey pain. But what had caused all this?

Overhead were hundreds of feet of solid rock and earth. Yet that slow, writhing smoke had suddenly burst from out the solid earth!

The words of Wilson, the foreman, drummed in Marlowe's brain. Reilly's screams had faded "like—like he was bein' dragged down...." And then, for no logical reason, Marlowe felt the blood in his veins grow thin and cold. The pain, the burning sensation was almost unbearable now on his cheek. Tears began to form in his eyes, and he stepped back through the smoke to the clearer air.

Fighting to keep his hands steady, to keep from screaming with the torture of his pain, Marlowe stepped to the edge of the creek, knelt by it and placed the light on the rock beside him. Focusing its beam across the oily black water, he splashed some on his face.

The ice-cold drops soothed the pain.

The gun still tight in his right hand, finger on the trigger, Marlowe straightened. Whatever the strange, invisible thing that had struck silently, leaving terrific pain in its wake, whatever the invisible monster that had twisted and contorted and killed Reilly, it might strike again at any moment. Horribly, painfully, it might strike from the darkness, to leave him to a tortured, twisted corpse!

"It's *got* to be here somewhere!" he spoke the words aloud, desperately. "It can't dive through solid rock—" And then Marlowe started abruptly, and air hissed through his thin, hard lips. For Reilly's corpse was naked—yet there were no clothes in the vault!

He stood up, looked closely at the body. It was horribly swollen; the face a bloated mask of agony; the cheeks had puffed until the eyes were almost invisible.

The light moved over the rest of the body. The legs, arms, abdomen, were also swollen grotesquely, horribly. And this was the death that had struck at him—Ken Marlowe! The hair along the nape of Marlowe's neck rose stiffly and he felt his flesh grow prickly. "Good God!" he said, his voice a hoarse whisper. *"God!"*

Slowly Marlowe bent, placed the flash so that the stream of light fell on the dead man's face and shoulders. He stuck the gun in his right coat pocket. Then he caught the man by the wrists, twisted, and the body straightened on its back. Straddling the man's legs. Marlowe jerked, ducked his right shoulder. The body sprawled across his shoulder.

With his free hand, Marlowe picked up the flash and headed toward the mouth of the abandoned shaft. His cheek rested against the cold, clammy side of the corpse.

The light stabbed through the absolute darkness, lay white against the uneven floor of the shaft, wavered across the black walls, as Marlowe went toward the main tunnel.

A GRAY blur of light marked the mouth of the tunnel. As Marlowe walked toward it the light grew brighter, more clearly outlined. He saw the miners standing in the white glare of the sunlight beyond the mouth of the tunnel. Frightened faces with wide, white eyes peered intently toward the shaft-mouth.

Marlowe stepped into the glare, the corpse across his shoulder. The men jerked instinctively back and eyes bulged toward Marlowe. Stepping across the tracks Marlowe stopped, bent over and slid the body from his shoulder to the ground. Crim and Brady sprinted toward him from the little office. Behind them came Wilson.

"Well," Marlowe said quietly, "so there actually was something to Wilson's story!"

For a moment neither man answered, but stood staring, shocked faces turned toward the body at their feet. Behind them Wilson moved closer slowly, peering with wide, terrified eyes.

Crim stepped across the body, beside which Brady had knelt, and looked closely at Marlowe. "What the hell happened to your face? It's got the strangest red markings—"

Brady stood up abruptly. "This man," he said nudging the body with the toe of his shoe, "has been choked!"

"What?" Marlowe snapped, ignoring Crim's question about his face. He dropped to his knees beside Ed Reilly. Around the man's throat and under his chin ran a dark welt, visible even after the abnormal swelling.

"Look at the way the eyes roll back," Brady said. "That's the way they do when they're strangled."

Slowly Marlowe got to his feet, still looking at the body. The lines of his jaw were hard, and the red spots on his cheek burned brightly against his dark skin. He raised cold eyes toward Brady, and then suddenly turned.

Pushing his way through the miners, came a tall, slender man. His wavy blond hair was slightly tousled, and a troubled curiosity showed in his deep blue eyes. Everet Starlin had been looking over Southern Coal for several days, but he had made no definite offer to buy. He had been in the office twice to talk the matter over with the owners, but he had always been evasive as to whom he represented.

A smile curled his full, sensuous lips as he looked up from the corpse to Marlowe. "He looks like he got caught in a hornet's nest," Starlin said. "And you do too, for that matter. What happened? Why is he naked?"

Marlowe looked again at the corpse without answering. A sudden light flickered in his eyes. Starlin's shoes and the cuffs of his trousers were wet and blackened with coal dust!

The light died in Marlowe's eyes and he raised his face toward the buyer. "I'll be damned if I know," he said matter-of-factly. "He was naked when I found him. And his clothes had disappeared."

Starlin chuckled softly and his blue eyes danced. "Sounds like a good ghost story," he said.

"Yeah," Marlowe said. "It does. Only—it isn't. Not by a damned sight!"

He stepped across the body, headed toward the office.

"One minute, Mr. Marlowe," Earle Brady snapped.

Marlowe wheeled, and Brady glared at him with granite eyes. He shifted his gaze quickly to Crim, to the huddled miners listening intently, and back to Marlowe. "When I come out tomorrow," his voice clicked with cold precision, "my offer will be fifty thousand less than what I offered today. We can't pay exhorbitant prices for mines where there'll be trouble getting labor. Good-bye, Mr. Marlowe."

He nodded his head curtly at Crim, stepped to the tram line, went briskly down it toward the lot where he had left his automobile.

Marlowe jammed his hands hard into his pockets, the muscles about his jaw knotting into tight lumps. From troubled eyes he stared a long, silent moment at Crim. And then he laughed harshly.

"Well—that's that!" he bit out. "But I'm damned if I either understand it—or like it!"

Without another word he turned and hard-heeled back toward the office.

CHAPTER TWO

DEATH STALKS THE DARK!

BEFORE A small mirror inside the frame shack, Marlowe studied the red welts on his face. Most of the pain had left, although a slight stinging sensation remained. He bathed the spots carefully with antiseptic, and was patting a towel against his face when Crim stepped inside the office and closed the door softly behind him.

Crim's round, pleasant face had gone suddenly hard and his eyes were a steely blue. He strode to his desk, flung one leg over a corner of it.

"Now what the hell's all this about, Ken?" he snapped. "The damn thing's getting me. And God knows it isn't helping us sell this mine!"

Marlowe turned slowly, shrugged his broad shoulders. "Just what I said, Crim—and a little more." He explained in detail his experience in the abandoned shaft.

When he had finished, Crim did not answer. He sat, staring down at the floor, the tips of his fingers drumming a soft tattoo on the desk-top. Then he said abruptly: "I wish to heaven I knew something about this bird Starlin. He waited until you had gone and then started asking me a lot of fool questions. He said he'd been down by Warrior Creek in one of the little mines down there."

Marlowe did not answer. He crossed the office, jerked his coat from the chair back and slipped into it. He stopped with his hand around the door-knob, turned and faced Crim.

"Listen," he snapped. "You remember what Wilson said several days ago about this Ahao Larvki, the fortune teller, telling some of the Negroes they were going to get hurt in this mine? Well, If I remember, Ed Reilly was one of those he warned. Now how did he figure that out?"

Crim ceased drumming on the table. His blue eyes twinkled as he looked at Marlowe. "What are you doing, growing superstitious on me? But if you want to ask him what's down the abandoned shaft, you can come with me tonight. He's holding a seance and I promised my fiancée I'd take her. He's supposed to be good—if you like that sort of thing."

Marlowe touched his fingers softly to his right cheek, took them away and fumbled in his pocket for a cigarette. "Thanks, but I'm going to call on Ed's widow for a few minutes tonight and tell her she'll get her insurance all right, and any food she wants before then." Marlowe stuck the cigarette between his lips, ran a match down the door sill, fanned it across the end of the cigarette. "I reckon after all it doesn't take any deep crystal gazing to tell that somebody is likely to get hurt in a coal mine."

He turned slowly, stepped into the little yard about the office. Every man had disappeared. The late afternoon sun fell obliquely on the swollen shape beneath a blanket at the tunnel's mouth. Ed Reilly's distorted body lay there, like a sinister portent of doom.

THE door of Ed Reilly's house was open when Marlowe braked his car to a halt on the narrow street that ran before it. Through the open door lamp light spilled into the dark yard. Two Negroes stood in the doorway. There were evidently more inside.

But the voice that poured through the open door was not that of an Alabama Negro. It was crisp, hard, and high-pitched. Ringing, fervent, the words made Marlowe's eyes grow hard and narrow.

"If you want to protect yourselves, if you want to keep your husbands and yourself from being murdered and tortured as this poor woman's husband was murdered, you've got to organize...." The man's voice went high and shrill. Marlowe recognized it. Bill Daniels, a labor agitator.

Ken Marlowe leaped to the doorway, thrust the men aside. On the far side of the room stood a white man. He was a tall, gaunt man, and the rose of consumption flamed in his cheeks. Between Marlowe and the agitator sat several Negro women and others were ranged around the walls.

As Marlowe flung hard, level eyes around the room, Bill Daniels stopped talking abruptly. And then Marlowe's eyes came to focus on a slim figure near the fireplace. Standing near the lamp on the mantelpiece, yellow light making bronze fires in her Titian hair, stood a girl.

THE girl's face was flushed about the cheeks. Full, scarlet lips and dark eyes set far apart gave the face an incredible beauty. A dark dress clung to the full curves of her body. She straightened consciously under his gaze, walked across the room to the man against the far wall.

With an effort, Marlowe took his eyes from the girl, and quietly asked: "Which one of you is Ed's wife?"

A stout, elderly negress stood up. Her eyes were red and in her hand she held a damp square of cloth. "I am Ed Reilly's wife. Me an' Ed, we—" She began to sob.

"I'm sorry about what happened today," Marlowe said. "None of us know how it happened, but we'll find out. I came to tell you that you'll get your insurance money from the company all right. And if you need any food or rent money before then, just come up to the office and see me."

The woman dabbed her eyes with the damp cloth. "I 'spect I'll need me some rent money, cause Ed—" She began to sob again.

"All right. You'll get it." Marlowe's eyes swept the rest of the room, stopped on the white man and girl standing silent against the far wall.

"And you can put in your speech," Marlowe said, his voice hard, "there'll be no more murders in that mine. We won't put the workers back in the mine until we find out what—what the thing was. We never had trouble there before, and we won't have it now."

The gaunt man took a step forward and his voice blazed. "Why didn't you make sure before you sent a man in there to be murdered that the shaft was safe? When you deliberately let your men be killed, it's murder! And you're the murderer!"

Ken Marlowe's lips jerked thin. Moving on the balls of his feet, he crossed the center of the room. His hands were knotted fists, waist high.

A crimson flush in his gaunt cheeks, the man stepped to meet him.

Then like a dark wind the girl swept forward, past the man. She stopped in front of Marlowe and her eyes were dancing flames. "You heard what my father called you! Murderer! You let your men be killed in your mines, and now…." Her voice broke suddenly, went low. "You want to fight him because he told you the truth—and he's—he's sick."

The hard lines around Marlowe's mouth relaxed. He started to speak but the man had caught his daughter by the arm, pulled her behind him. "Be quiet, Ellen," he said softly. "This is my affair."

In the gaunt lines about the man's mouth and in the almost crazy light that burned in his eyes Marlowe recognized the sincere fanatic. The man was certain he was right, and would go to any extreme to uphold his cause.

Abruptly the man began to cough, and the hard light went out of Marlowe's eyes. "I want you to know, sir," he said, "that what I told you a moment ago is true. I won't put the men back to work until I am certain they are safe."

The man bowed slightly. "I hope you are sincere. But there's another question I'd like to ask you, here, in front of your employees. Why…."

He halted, his mouth still open, his eyes growing suddenly large. A soft, thumping noise sounded in the chimney. Marlowe spun on his heel. His eyes flicked across the faces of the miners to where the yellow glow of the lamp glinted strangely.

Something was sliding down the chimney, thumping at the sides. Soot fell in black flakes on the open hearth.

Then into the open fireplace slid black feet and legs. The feet slid downward, touched the hearth. The knees, barely visible below the top of the fireplace, bent slightly, caught against the brick, stopped.

Air burst from Ken Marlowe's lungs. "God!" he breathed.

The naked feet and legs were puffed and grotesque; horribly swollen.

A Negro woman screamed wildly, flung up her hands, smashed over backward in her chair. With hoarse shouts the men leaped for the door, splintering chairs as they flung them against the wall. Barely conscious of the mad rush which shook the floor under them, they stared with popping eyeballs at the swollen legs and feet propped in the empty fireplace.

Before he moved, Marlowe knew there was no life in those grotesque legs and ankles. Knew that the thing which had killed Ed Reilly had also killed this man!

With one stride Marlowe reached the chimney, caught the ankles, pulled.

Soot burst into the fireplace, swirled along the hearth. The body of a naked man fell with a soggy noise into the room. The head clicked back against the bricks of the chimney with a loud cracking sound. It was an old Negro, his face swollen almost beyond recognition. Marlowe's tongue clicked against his teeth with a hissing sound. It was another of his miners!

Two of his men now had been tortured to death—and the shrieks of one and the body of the other had been used to frighten the rest of his laborers.

Now it would be impossible to put them back to work in the mines until this fiendishness had been completely cleared up or forgotten. What could anyone hope to gain by these barbarous murders?

Behind him Marlowe heard the girl gasp.

Spinning, Marlowe stared at Bill Daniels who stood watching him with fevered eyes. He had been attempting to stir up trouble among the laborers, asking them to strike. Well—this would get the men out of the mines!

LIKE a man flung from a catapult Ken Marlowe hurtled out the door. There, he twisted around to look at the roof of the little house. The chimney ran up the right wall and against it leaned an old ladder. Marlowe sprinted to the back of the house. Nothing there.

Some man had brought this body here, climbed that ladder, and flung the body down the chimney. There was no other way possible. "The dead don't walk," Marlowe whispered under his breath.

A number of footprints showed dully in the gray blanket of dust made visible by his flash. Even among the mingling of prints the marks of heavy-heeled shoes were plain at the foot of the ladder.

Marlowe whistled soundlessly. He flung the finger of light along the tracks, tracing them. A double set of footprints led from where the weeds of a vacant lot joined the small yard—and then the tracks returned.

He switched off the light and stood, body tense, staring into the darkness. For fifty yards the weed-grown lot lay flat, empty. Beyond the lot a serrated line of trees showed black against the graying sky. A full moon crouched just under the horizon, and would soon be swaying up into the sky.

Marlowe started on a run across the lot toward the trees, his fingers clenching the butt of his pocketed automatic.

"The man must be mad, stark mad!" The words beat into Marlowe's brain as he ran. That part of the country had seen crazy murderers before, but never one who followed this inhuman, fantastic method.

Yet, even as his lips formed the words Marlowe knew that he was chasing no insane killer. There was some monstrous plan back of the whole macabre affair. Why did it always strike when there were crowds of Negroes about? When Marlowe himself was nearby?

Marlowe slowed down and stepped slowly into the fringe of trees. The ground here was a pool of ebony shadows cast by foliage overhead. He stood for a long moment, the little muscles back of his ears taut as he strained for sound.

Then, spinning silently, the gun leaping from his pocket, he flattened himself against a tree trunk. A dark shadow was coming across the lot toward him.

Marlowe slid along the tree until the trunk was between him

and the sound of the running steps. Eyes probing the darkness he saw a blacker shadow swaying in the flat darkness of the weed-grown lot. It seemed to move with a floating, rocking motion, as though it were being drawn through the air, but he could hear the sound of shoes on the hard-baked earth, the swish of cloth against weeds.

The gun moved slowly, came chest high, centered on the dark figure halfway between the trees and the dull spots of light that marked the miners' cabins. The crook of Marlowe's forefinger rested hard against the trigger. A full moon rocked one edge above the horizon, and gray light seeped across the weed-grown lot.

MARLOWE'S lips broke their thin line and air pushed into his lungs. His finger went lax on the trigger. "God!" he breathed. "I almost shot her!"

In the moonlight he could see the pale blur of Ellen Daniels' face. He stuck the gun in his pocket, stepped from behind the tree. The girl saw him move, stopped in her tracks, gasping.

"What are you doing here?" he demanded.

"Oh!" Her breath came in a long sigh of relief. "You frightened me."

Marlowe stepped close to her, stood looking down into her face. "Why did you come out here?" he repeated gruffly.

"I—I—" she dropped her eyes. "I thought you were someone else."

Sickening fear touched Marlowe's heart. Surely the girl could not be connected with this ghoulish business. Marlowe asked: "Who did you think I was?"

For a moment the girl did not answer. Then she raised her eyes squarely to Marlowe's. "My father."

An electrical thrill tingled through Marlowe, but he kept his voice steady. "Your father? I left him in the house with you."

Hesitantly the girl looked down at her laced fingers. "If you haven't seen him, I'll go back," she said.

Marlowe caught her by the shoulders. "Why did you think I was your father? Where did he go?"

"I don't know. He ran out of the house right after you. He said he was going to look for whoever dropped that—that body down the chimney. I didn't want to stay in there—alone. I went out in the yard. There was someone going this way and I thought it was father, so I followed."

Marlowe laughed, a short, harsh sound. He had stood still, waiting for the killer—and had let the murderer escape. Disappointment was bitter in his mouth. He had been so close on the heels of this fiend and of the solution of this grisly mystery, and now he had let it slip away from him!

The girl's voice was soft. "I thought you were very nice back there, and I'm sorry for what I said. But I'm—I'm worried about father. He's not well anyway. Lately he's been hanging around your mine. Going out there at night and coming home all muddy and wet. I wish I knew what the trouble was."

Marlowe felt the corners of his mouth twitch. He remembered the wild, fanatical look in the man's eyes. "You say he comes home all wet?" He tried to keep his voice cool, matter-of-fact.

"Yes. There's something—something terrible going to happen. I can feel it in the very air. That—that man falling down the chimney tonight—the other one that was killed in the mine today. I don't know what it all means, or what father has to do with it, but I'm afraid. He's been carrying a gun ever since he went to see that spiritualist. He never did that before. And yesterday—"

Her voice snapped and her hands clutched suddenly at Marlowe's coat.

Too late Marlowe heard the snakelike hiss above his head. It brushed his face, sullied about his neck, tightened. It jerked backward, cutting off his breath, flinging him headlong to the earth.

Marlowe hit the ground writhing and tried to struggle up again, but the dark shadow drove him back, forced him down. He caught a short glimpse of ferocious eyes glaring from behind a black mask, the glint of moonlight on metal.

A terrified scream burst in the night air, tore at Marlowe's ears. He heard Ellen Daniels stumbling backward. His gun caught in his coat pocket as he tore at it.

Something cracked loudly over his eyes. Dark shadows whirled dizzily about him, crashed into his brain. And he was out.

CHAPTER THREE

"SO SOON A CORPSE!"

HIS HEAD ached fiercely and little lights danced before his eyes. Marlowe rolled over, groaned, strained his eyelids. He was lying inside the fringe of trees. He pushed his hands against the leafy earth, sat up. The ground wavered slightly, settled. Marlowe staggered to his feet, cursing bitterly.

"Walked into their trap like a damn half-wit," he said aloud. He stuck his hand in his pocket; the gun was gone. He stepped to the edge of the trees and looked across the vacant lot.

His brain cleared swiftly as remembrance stabbed him. Ellen had screamed just before he was hit over the head. He had heard her stumbling. "God!" he whispered. "They must have got her!"

He started across the vacant lot, his fists clenched into hard mauls. He was halfway to Ed Reilly's before his fury cooled enough for him to realize that he had no idea where to look for the girl and her captors.

A dozen frightened-eyed negroes were grouped on the sidewalk in front of Ed Reilly's house. They began to draw away when Marlowe swung around the side of the house and went toward them.

"Listen," the mine owner barked, "have you seen that girl or her father? Or anyone else around here since—since I left?"

Dead silence answered him while the men huddled together. Then one of them spoke. "Naw, sir. Us ain't seen nobody, ain't heard nobody. Ain't nobody been around here."

"All right." Marlowe stepped across the sidewalk to his car, slid in, threw the switch. On the first corner he swung to the right toward Underwood Avenue, driving slowly.

Abruptly Marlowe's hands closed hard over the wheel. There was one chance left! Ellen had said something about her father going to the spiritualist—and Ahao Larvki had predicted the death of some of the men in the mine. Perhaps....

Marlowe laughed deep in his throat. Hell! Probably wasn't even the same spiritualist. But he jammed his foot down on the gas. It was the only possible chance, and he wouldn't overlook it.

He turned off Underwood and went down Eighth Street toward Avenue F, then up the Avenue, running fast. Unconsciously Marlowe's teeth ground together as an appalling vision of the girl's soft body, twisted and swollen, flashed through his mind.

Why, if this fiend was so willing to murder and kidnap, had he not killed Marlowe when he lay unconscious? Perhaps he had believed him dead. Well, that was one mistake!

Marlowe tugged his car into a small side street. At the first corner a dull arclight glowed and candle flies circling it threw dancing shadows on the dusty street. Just beyond the intersection Marlowe pulled his car to the curb, stopped, got out.

There were only two houses in the block, both on the right, one on each corner and separated by a vacant lot overgrown with weeds. It was the house on the far corner, set back from the street, in which Ahao Larvki communed with the spirits.

MARLOWE started diagonally across the vacant lot toward the soothsayer's house. There were no cars in front, but if Crim and his fiancée, Edith Waters, were here, their car was probably parked on the other side of the house.

Tall weeds swished against Marlowe's trousers legs as he walked. The moon was higher now and he could see the bare outline of the house, the blank, blind windows except for one far back where a tiny slit of green light showed.

Marlowe reached the side of the house, slipped along it toward the lighted window. Standing on tip-toe Marlowe put his eye to the slit of light. Heavy curtains hung inside the window several inches away from the sill. The light slipped through between them, but in such a way that Marlowe, standing outside, could see nothing of the interior.

Marlowe cursed silently and turned back toward the front of the house. There, he stopped at the first window.

For a long moment he stood motionless, his ears pricked to catch the slightest noise. The house might have been a grave for all the sound that came from it.

The window was about chin-high. Marlowe caught the screen between lean, hard fingers; pushed. It slid up silently. He pushed on the window and it moved upwards on oiled pulleys.

Ken Marlowe rested strong hands on the window sill. His knees bent slightly, then he jumped, and crawled into the room.

The room where he stood was almost pitch dark. The window showed a gray-blue square against the moonlight. To the right was a door beneath which showed a slit of the sickly green light he had seen from outside. With outstretched hands, Marlowe inched his way toward it.

A woman's nervous laughter jarred through the dead silence and Marlowe's hand snaked for his coat pocket, stopped as he remembered his gun was gone. A man's deep voice murmured words unintelligible to the mine operator half crouched there in the darkness. Then a grim smile twisted the corners of his mouth. His nerves were getting jumpy. One of Larvki's clients had laughed, nothing else.

Through Marlowe's mind flashed that horrible moment when the invisible thing had struck him, the writhing smoke bursting from solid rock, the terrific pain that had flashed from nowhere to strike at his face and the noose that had come out of the darkness to snatch the breath from him.

The grim smile still twisting his lips, Marlowe edged toward the light. In the darkness he made out folding glass doors and a few inches beyond them a heavy black curtain through which the light fell.

Folding his hand around the door-knob he twisted softly, pulled the door slightly ajar. He knelt, caught one side of the curtain between the thumb and forefinger of his left hand, pulled it slightly back.

The room beyond was lit with a ghastly, dim green light. At the far end an open fire burned, its yellow and red flames dancing strangely in the sickly green of the concealed lighting. And to the right of the fire, in deep shadows, sat a man dressed in long black robes. Near Marlowe, with their backs half turned toward him, five persons sat in straight chairs. He recognized Crim and Edith Waters. The next couple he did not know. And in the fifth chair, leaning tensely forward, was Everet Starlin.

ABRUPTLY the man near the fire stood up, walked into the center of the room where the light was brighter. He was short, with wide shoulders from which his black robe fell in rippling folds to the floor. His face was dark, with thick lips; heavy, but with well shaped features. Hawaiian, or South Sea Islander, Marlowe thought.

His voice rolled musically when he spoke, but there was a mystic, strained note in it. "I am ready now for the Mr. Crim's and the Mr. Starlin's questions," he said. "I will take them both at the same time. Write them as the others have."

Staring through the curtains Marlowe watched Crim and Starlin take paper and fountain pens from their pockets. Crim was writing on the back of one of the company envelopes. As the other couple turned to watch Crim with wide eyes, Marlowe could see their faces. A young couple, probably mill folk.

The questions written, both men, evidently following directions Larvki had given the others, folded the notes in small squares, put them in envelopes, sealed the envelopes. Larvki stepped back to the fire, picked up a pair of tongs, came back and held them open first before Crim and then Starlin, letting each man place his note between the tongs. Then without having ever touched the envelopes, he carried the tongs back to the open fire, thrust the envelopes into the blaze.

The flames licked at the paper, shot up higher. The paper curled blackly as it burned, fell in tiny fragments into the fire.

WHEN it had finished burning Larvki set the tongs beside the fire, took his seat again. As he sat down the tong slipped on the hearth, fell with a ringing clatter. Larvki leaned forward, straightened the tongs, his features twisting strangely.

Kneeling there, peering into the ghostly, lighted room, Marlowe felt cold fear tingle along his back. Edith Waters' fingers twisted nervously in front of her. Crim and Starlin were also leaning forward, staring at the man in the shadows, tense, expectant.

Marlowe's eyes fastened hard on Larvki. He wondered how the man was going to fake answers to questions he could not possibly know. Suddenly Larvki gasped, stood up straight in the shadows. His voice leaped through the room, talking swiftly in that strained, far-away tone. "You are advised to sell your property at once, Mr. Crim, and at any thing you can get for it. There will always be trouble in that mine. One man has died—no! I see two dead bodies! And there are the ghostly outlines of others yet to come." The voice died abruptly, like the sudden end of a bell's ringing and taut silence held the room. Marlowe's fingers had gone hard, clutching the curtain.

How could this man know of what had happened in the mine? How could he know of the second death when the papers did not know, when Crim did not know—when Marlowe himself had not known an hour before? There were only two possible answers. Either the man *was* able to see spirits, or....

Ahao Larvki was speaking again, and the dead, far-away voice held an excited quiver. "Mr. Crim, you have a partner, a business associate. He is nearby—and in great danger. I see the outline of his form near those of the dead men. I see his automobile wrecked!"

Marlowe felt a chill wave sweep along his spine and his heart clogged in his throat. Could this man know he was nearby? This man who had predicted the death of the miners—now predicted the death of Ken Marlowe! What supernatural power did he have that enabled him to read messages that had been burned?

Marlowe's lips twisted grimly. He'd know something about it before this forecasted death came true!

He tensed himself to fling the curtain aside, but stopped as the voice of Ahao Larvki came again with a wild rush.

"And you, Mr. Starlin, your question has to do with the same thing. But you will never know. It is good that Mr. Crim did not seek so much information; even now perhaps he will not escape. But—" the voice dropped to a sound like the soft beating of wings in the air—"I see your body among the dead, Mr. Starlin. So soon, so very soon, nothing but a lifeless corpse!"

EVERET STARLIN surged to his feet and Marlowe could see his big frame trembling. Then he laughed hoarsely. "You may be right, Prophet," he sneered. "But before I bump off I think I'll take a look at those tongs you burn the notes with." He strode past Larvki to the fireplace, picked up the tongs.

Through the narrow part in the curtains Marlowe stared at Everet Starlin, watched him go over the tongs minutely. Finally, holding them by the head, he raised baffled eyes toward Ahao Larvki. "They look all right," he admitted grudgingly.

His inscrutable expression never changing, Larvki said, "If you doubt they are sound, jar them on the hearth. If there is nothing wrong, perhaps you will believe us."

Twice Everet Starlin rapped the iron tongs on the hearth. The dull sounds rang with muffled echoes against the curtained walls. Then, his face suddenly growing livid, he dropped them. He staggered slightly as he went back to his chair, slumped into it. "Is there any one else who doubts?" the mystic said quietly.

Marlowe heard the words break from his lips before he knew he was going to speak. "Yes."

He flung the curtain aside, leaped into the room, straight toward Larvki. The mill girl screamed shrilly as she saw Marlowe's face, a ghastly color under the green light. He went toward Larvki, moving on the balls of his feet, fingers claw-like at his side.

The medium sprang back, startled. "Who—who are you?" he cried.

Marlowe caught him by the shoulders with lean, hard fingers. They were broad, muscular shoulders, but Marlowe saw the grimace of pain on the swarthy face as his fingers tightened. "You ought to ask a spirit," Marlowe snarled. "But I'll tell you. I'm the man you said was nearby and going to get killed. And I want to find out how you know so much." The man flinched as Marlowe's fingers dug like steel hooks into his shoulders.

Frank Crim had jumped to his feet as Marlowe stepped into the room. Now he put a hand on his associate's arm. "What the hell, Ken? Where did you come from?"

Before Marlowe answered the spiritualist spoke, his voice cool. "If the gentleman doubts that I speak true, let him look behind him—at Mr. Starlin."

Flinging the medium from him, Marlowe spun on his heel. Everet Starlin was doubled over in his chair, his arms clasped about his belly. His face was dead white and against the pallor of his cheeks the flush of his lips showed strangely. His mouth was partially open and his breath came in wheezing gasps as he twisted in agony on his chair.

The mill girl had turned to look at him. Her mouth flew open, lips trembling before the scream burst from them. She staggered from her seat, clutching frantically at the young man with her.

With one leap Marlowe reached Starlin, caught his shoulders. "What's the trouble?" he rasped.

Starlin struggled for breath. "Get me out of here," he gasped. "A hospital! I—I'm sick!"

Everet Starlin was a big man, but Marlowe caught him up in his arms like a baby, brushed through the curtains and out the door. Moonlight made the steps a gray blur. Marlowe raced down them, along the sidewalk toward his car.

His arms were aching with the weight of the man before he reached the car and slid him on the back seat. Leaping under the wheel Marlowe flipped the switch, jabbed the starter and raced toward the Hillman Hospital. Tires whined as Marlowe pulled his car into Twentieth Street, screamed again as he jammed on the brakes outside the emergency door of the Hillman.

Two porters were running down the walk before Marlowe swung out of the car. Without questions they dragged Starlin from the back seat, carried him up the walk. And Ken Marlowe, his jaw set, followed.

In the emergency room a white-coated interne jerked open Starlin's coat and shirt, put a stethoscope to the man's chest. For a moment he leaned over him, then turned slowly to Marlowe.

"The man's dead," he said quietly.

CHAPTER FOUR

LARUKI & CO.

KEN MARLOWE stood looking into the doctor's eyes unbelievingly; afraid to believe what he knew to be true. Everet Starlin was dead! The soothsayer had said he would die—and, apparently healthy a few minutes before, he had died. And the fortune-teller had said that he, Marlowe, would die soon. He felt his heart freeze in his chest. Three men before him had been marked for death by this seer; and three men had died, all of them horribly. Now he was the fourth....

Marlowe fought to keep his voice steady. "How did he die, Doctor? What was wrong with him?"

The interne moved slow eyes to the body on the operating table, then back to Marlowe. "You'll have to tell me something about the case. When did he grow sick.? How did he say he felt?"

"He was just sitting still," Marlowe said softly. He was afraid to tell the doctor too much; anger was flaming in him and he didn't want the police holding him for questioning. Not if what he suspected was true. "Suddenly he grabbed his belly," Marlowe went on. "He said he was sick. That's all. I rushed him here."

The interne rubbed the fingers of his right hand hard across his chin. "Of course I can't say certainly without an autopsy, but the indications are that he had ptomaine poisoning. It seldom strikes so suddenly, but it has been known to do so. Do you know what he had been eating?"

Marlowe shook his head. He said, his voice heavy: "Is it possible to give a person ptomaine poisoning any way except through their food?"

The doctor's hand froze on his chin. "What do you mean?" His eyes snapped.

Marlowe's mind was racing back over the things he had seen that night. He didn't want the cops now. He'd got himself into this thing and he'd get out alone, or not at all! "I don't mean anything in particular," he said softly. "I was just wondering."

The doctor, still watching him curiously, took his name and address and Starlin's name. As he drove away from in front of the hospital, he saw the interne standing on the sidewalk, taking down his license tag number. Marlowe smiled grimly. By the time the interne had made that autopsy and learned whatever he was going to learn, Marlowe would be ready for the cops—if they came.

He turned into Avenue F again and started down it. Marlowe uttered a sudden exclamation. It had flashed into his mind as he watched the doctor pressing his fingers against his chin.

"Damned crook," he muttered. "So that's the way Larvki read those burned notes! He simply clamped the tongs on the envelopes where they held the notes, so they wouldn't burn. Then when the tongs slipped down on the hearth and he straightened them, he picked up the notes, palmed them and read. Clever. Too damned clever."

Marlowe's knuckles whitened around the wheel. "And if he faked that...." he whispered aloud.

His brain was racing so that his eyes, staring straight ahead, did not see the big green automobile lurch from the shadows at the intersection of Eighth Street and the Avenue until it was almost on him. Furiously he jerked at the wheel. Tires screamed shrilly as the machine rocked to one side. The other car swerved, but not enough.

He felt the smash jar through his machine, fling it against the curb. The car rocked dangerously, came down on all four wheels, the front tire exploding like a shotgun.

Cursing, Marlowe cut off the motor. Well, the forecast wreck had happened all right, but Larvki had been wrong about the rest. He wasn't dead—yet! He pushed open a door, stepped out.

A red tail light was vanishing a block away on the Avenue.

Quickly, Marlowe looked over his car. The right rear fender

was crumpled against the tire, but could be pulled out. The left front tire was blown. He went to work on it, moving rapidly, and cursing through clenched teeth.

UNDER the arc light, a block from the house of Ahao Larvki, the circling candle flies threw weaving shadows that danced on the dusty street. Ken Marlowe braked his automobile to a halt just outside the dim circle of light, got out. Rapidly, he went down the unpaved sidewalk toward the house of the spiritualist.

As he went, feet thudding on the unpaved walk, his hands crushed into rocklike balls. Larvki had faked the note reading. Then he must have faked his predictions. And there was only one way! He was connected with this fiendish business! Marlowe straightened his fingers, knotted them again. At last he had something to work on, some chance to find what lay back of this.

When he saw the pale green glow sliding narrowly through the back window, Marlowe cut across the weed-grown lot. Outside the window he had entered some two hours earlier he stopped. The window was still raised. Once more he flipped himself in as he had done before, slid across the darkened room to the black curtains. Muffled words came through the closed doors. Marlowe slowly pulled the door open, pushed the curtains stealthily apart.

In the next room three masked men were grouped in front of the open fire. And standing facing them, her back to the fire, head high, eyes defiant, was Ellen Daniels! Marlowe's breath came in a slow hiss.

Black, hood-like masks, with narrow slits for eyes, hid the faces of the men, muffled their words as they spoke. One of them had the girl by the wrist. Marlowe saw her flinch slightly as the man tightened his grip.

"All right," the man said, "we're getting damned tired of playing with you. You know what your old man is doing—or trying to do. And that's what we want to know. So come clean, sister, and talk fast!" He wrenched her wrist.

Ken Marlowe swung his shoulders toward the curtain. Then he stopped. Hidden, he might learn the secret behind this murderous affair. What part did this girl and her fanatical father play?

"I've told you." she gasped. "I don't know what he's after. He never told me."

"Well, maybe you can guess," the man to the side of her sneered. His hand flicked out of the shadows toward her face, then dropped without touching her. Marlowe saw something glint in his fingers.

For a moment the girl stood perfectly still. Marlowe saw her eyes darken with fear and saw her lips quiver as she fought for control. Then she screamed.

She jerked both hands free, began to heat frantically at her face. The man at her side clamped his hands over her mouth and muffled her cries. Agony twisted her body. Yet the man's hand had never touched her!

Ken Marlowe hurled aside the curtains, dove toward the group like a mad man. The tall man spun to face him, his hand flashing toward his left shoulder. Marlowe's shoulder struck him, flinging him backward. They crashed into the man in the shadows, bowling him over like a tenpin, and all three smashed to the floor.

Twisting, Marlowe lashed out with his fist toward a mask, felt his knuckles jar on flesh and bone. He heard Ellen scream. He heaved his body to the right, rolling across the floor.

The roar of a gun jarred the room, echoed crashingly between the curtained walls. Leaping to his feet, Marlowe saw the man who was standing before the fire swing the gun to cover him, saw Ellen grasp the barrel. The gun roared.

With one sweep of his left hand Marlowe caught up a chair, drove forward holding it shield-like before him. The chair cracked into the gun, knocking it from the man's hand.

ELLEN screamed again, and Marlowe spun sideways, flinging the chair as he spun. The man he had tackled was on his knees, tugging at his gun. The chair struck him in the chest, hurling him backward.

The man before the fire dived for the gun on the floor. Marlowe kicked it viciously, and it skidded across the room toward the curtains. He grasped Ellen by the wrist, jerked her with him as he dived after the gun, shoved her through the curtains into the next room.

There was no time to look around. Marlowe flung himself sideways and down, hit the floor rolling, the gun in his hand. A gun thundered and he heard the thud of the bullet as it hit the wall over his head. Then he was on his knees, bringing up the pistol he had knocked from one of the masked men.

The room was empty.

Marlowe leaped to his feet. A dark stain of blood showed on the floor near the fireplace. The smear looked black in the shadows. Marlowe smiled grimly. One of the men's shots hadn't missed altogether. It had struck one of his confederates.

He heard a door at the back of the house slam. Flinging the curtain aside, Marlowe leaped into the next room, dived for the door. Something struck his legs and he crashed to the floor. Cursing the chair he had stumbled over, he staggered to his feet. felt for the door. His hands ran across the smooth walls frantically, found the knob, twisted. The door was locked.

Drawing back, Marlowe flung himself against the door, splintered the flimsy wood. Then he stopped, cursing. A half block away he heard a motor burst into action, the grinding of gears.

Standing where the curtains framed her in soft black folds, Ellen watched Marlowe come into the room. Three small red welts dotted her left cheek, and from them inflamed lines spider-webbed. Marlowe stopped before her, his eyes dark with anxiety. The girl put one hand gently to her cheek. "I don't know what happened," she said. "One of those men just waved his hand in front of me, and—and my face seemed to burst into flame. It doesn't hurt much now, but it's so weird, so strange, it frightens me."

Marlowe wheeled, went rapidly but carefully over the floor in front of the area where the girl had stood. And he found nothing.

He straightened, frowning, his eyes black fires. What devilish torture was this that could strike invisibly, vanish without leaving a trace, yet, given time, could work horrible, agonizing death? He thought of the two swollen, contorted bodies.

This wasn't the same thing that had struck Everet Starlin so suddenly and fiercely. Marlowe pulled his handkerchief from his pocket, stepped to the fireplace, picked up the tongs, holding them with the handkerchief. Starlin had held them by the top when Larvki had told him to strike them on the floor.

Marlowe rapped them on the hearth. A white needle flickered into the light on the top, vanished.

So! Pricked in the tough palm of his hand and with his mind fixed on the sound they would make, Starlin had not noticed the tiny prick. But why—why had they killed Starlin? What had been his connection with this wild nightmare of death and torture?

Marlowe turned to the girl, caught her hands in his. "We'd best get away from here before the police come; some neighbor has probably phoned them and there is too much to explain."

He led her through the curtains, through the darkened room, and out the front door where the full moon, high in the sky, spilled a white and mystic light along the dusty street.

The machine was where Marlowe had left it. He helped the girl in, walked around to the other side, crawled under the wheel.

"I—I'm very glad you weren't hurt in the wreck," the girl said.

Marlowe turned in his seat to face her, his eyes wide with amazement. "The wreck," he repeated. "How did you know there had been a wreck?"

"The man that knocked you over the head chloroformed me, took me to that house. When I came to I found two men with me. Later the third came in and he told the others he had run into you but hadn't turned your car over."

Marlowe laughed harshly as he started his car. "So it was all a fake, the whole business. Well, at last I know one man that's in it. Now all I've got to do," his smile was without humor, "is find Larvki and find his confederates and find the reason back of all these murders!"

As they backed under the street light and turned around, Marlowe saw the girl's wide, dark eyes fixed on him, saw their troubled look and the quiver on her lips. "I—I wish you wouldn't try to find out too much about this. It's dangerous, horrible," she said softly.

Marlowe's knuckles whitened on the wheel. "I'll be careful," he said grimly, "after I have a little talk with Ahao Larvki and company!"

CHAPTER FIVE

WRITHING DEATH

SLANTING SUNLIGHT fell in a golden bar through the window of the field office of Southern Coal, shone on the desk top and on Frank Crim's folded hands, but left his face in shadow as he stared up at his partner.

Both men were tired; they had been up since before dawn, had made their way to the little house recently occupied by Ahao Larvki. The house was empty, the front door standing ajar, just as Marlowe and Ellen had left it. The two men had gone at once to the deserted mine.

Marlowe's face was gray with fatigue and nervous strain as he met Crim's glance with troubled eyes.

"I wish to God," Marlowe was saying, "that Brady would come on out here! I want to see him."

"What's the rush?" Crim asked. "You interested in selling today?"

"No," Marlowe said slowly. "But I'm interested in the man who wants to buy. He wants to get the mine cheap, doesn't he?"

Crim laughed softly. "Of course, but so do a lot of other people. What are you driving at?"

Marlowe stuck his hand in his coat pocket, pulled out a cigarette, thrust it between his lips. He flicked a match with the end of his finger nail, touched the flame to the cigarette.

"I don't know exactly—yet. Give me time." He began to walk slowly back and forth across the office. A long gray ash grew on the cigarette and blue smoke trailed behind him.

For hours after he had taken Ellen home last night his brain had struggled vainly for some clue to this hellish business, for the reason back of it all. Why could anyone want to kill the men in his mine, torture them to a ghastly, horrible death? What connection had Ellen's father, the labor agitator, with this strange affair?

He lit another cigarette from the first, ground the butt under his toe. A third and fourth followed.

"Damn it!" Crim barked abruptly. "I wish to hell you'd get out of here to do your sherlocking. Not a man came to work today, and I sit here trying to figure out how to make a profit out of a mine we can't get anybody to work, and you keep pounding up and down the floor!"

Marlowe stopped, took the cigarette from his mouth, let the smoke crawl from between parted lips. "Okay," he said slowly. "You take care of the books. I'll get the mine to running again."

He went through the front door into the full sunlight. Outside he stood blinking against the bright daylight; he took a deep pull on his cigarette, blew the smoke against the big glass globe that circled the single light on an iron post in front of the office door. That was the only light left burning around the office at night.

In the bright morning the place had a strange quiet. There were no cars moving along the tram line, no checking man at the scales, not a human being in sight. On his way to the office that morning he had seen one of his miners, stopped to tell him there would be no work that day. The man had looked at him with fear-struck eyes.

"Naw, sir, dere ain't gonna be no work at dat mine fur me. Naw, sir, Ah ain't even livin' over heah no more. I'se movin' to Fairfiel'!" And the Negro had shuffled away, with quick, nervous steps.

MARLOWE'S eyes moved along the tram line to the mouth of the mine and stopped. Standing in front of the mine, the sunshine a golden fire burning in her hair, was Ellen Daniels. Marlowe went across the little yard toward her.

She heard his steps on the dust-covered ground and turned. "I'm glad you're here," she said quickly.

Looking down at her Marlowe felt again the sheer power of her beauty. "What's the trouble?" he demanded. "You look worried." He wondered what she was doing at the mouth of the tunnel which led to this macabre, underground mystery.

"Father came out here last night, and then again early this morning. He went down—down there. I couldn't stop him. He should have come out a long while ago, but he hasn't. I—I'm afraid…."

Marlowe put his hands on her shoulders, felt the soft warmth of her flesh under his fingers. He tried to make his voice steady. "I don't think anything could have happened to your father." The words were heavy in his throat and he could see that Ellen knew he was lying. "I'll go down and look for him," he added.

Her lips opened slightly, stiffened, while wild fear leaped to her eyes. "Listen!" she gasped. "What's that?"

A faint, wailing, unearthly sound had stirred the black air of the tunnel. So faint it was Marlowe could not be certain he had heard it, yet he knew what had caused it, and the blood in his veins went thin and cold. It was the torn, agonized shriek of a man in unbearable pain.

Marlowe caught the girl by the arm, jerked her away from the tunnel mouth. He sprinted for the office and as he ran he heard the girl behind him.

Dashing through the open door Marlowe skidded to a halt beside his desk, jerked open the drawer. A gun lay where he had put it that morning, but the flashlight was gone.

He swore, sticking the gun in his pocket. He remembered now that Crim had said last night he wanted to take the flash home to work on his car. Marlowe whirled toward Crim's desk but his partner had stepped out. Beside the door was a lantern. Marlowe leaped to it, snatched it up, lit it.

Just outside the door Marlowe paused, wrenched the big globe from around the light on the iron pillar. He put it up to his head; it was big enough to slip over.

Ellen Daniels caught him by the hand. "I'm going with you," she said, her voice husky.

Marlowe took the globe from his head, said savagely: "No! Get in there and wait, I'll be back—with your father." He started at a run toward the mouth of the mine.

The girl came running after him. Marlowe whirled. "Damn it," he barked. "Go back. There's no telling what's in that hole. And you.... I...."

She caught at his coat with both hands. "Don't you see?" she begged. "It's my—*my* father. I've *got* to go! If you won't take me, I'll follow!"

HOLDING the globe in one hand, the lantern in the other, Marlowe gazed at the girl for a split second, pride and fear for her clashing in his eyes. Dark terror showed in her face but her chin was held firmly high.

"All right," Marlowe said, "if you've got to come...." Dropping the lantern he leaped past her, tore the screen from the window of the office, ripped the frame from it. Quickly he bent it box shaped, came back and dropped it over her head. He picked up the lantern.

"I don't know what it is down there," he said, "but it hits at the bare parts of the body."

At the mouth of the tunnel he slipped the large globe over his own head. Lantern in one hand, gun in the other, he plunged into the darkness, Ellen Daniels close beside him.

The lantern threw a large circle of yellow light around their feet, but ahead the darkness pressed like a gigantic wall about to crash down on them. The tram tracks glinted in the light which splashed about their feet. Two yards ahead tracks and light vanished as if the earth had swallowed them.

Marlowe could feel his heart hammering against his ribs as they went down the tunnel. Yesterday he had come down this same way, wondering what lay at the end. Now he knew that death and writhing torture awaited them at the mouth of the abandoned shaft.

Their steps made tiny whispering sounds in the thick coal dust. In the dead stillness of the tunnel the noises seemed to grow and to echo like dead voices from the narrow walls.

Marlowe caught the rim of the globe with the hand that held

the lantern, lifted it from over his head. The girl stood holding the screen in her hands.

"What is it, Ken?" Her voice trembled, went quiet, and there was no sound except for the quick hissing of her breath.

"I want you to go back," Marlowe husked. "You've got no business down here. It's...."

Marlowe could feel the girl's hand clutching at his arm. "I *am* afraid," she whispered. "Horribly afraid. I—I feel that something terrible, something ghastly is going to happen. But—" and her hand tightened on Marlowe's arm—"I've *got* to go. If father's hurt, if he's—" Her voice broke sharply.

Marlowe raised the lantern so that the light fell full in the girl's face. Terror showed in the wide, dark eyes. "I've got to go, Ken," she repeated.

For a moment Marlowe held the lantern high, gazed into the girl's face. A calm fierceness seemed to band Marlowe with steel, and his fingers crushed hard around the butt of the automatic. By God! He'll see that nothing happened to this girl! If anything happened to her, he, Ken Marlowe, would wreck the thing even if it vanished where the smoke had come from—into the solid earth, and he had to tear the rocks apart!

Marlowe's voice was a low whisper when he spoke. "When we get out of here, Ellen, I—" He felt her hand tremble on his arm, knew that she understood.

He slipped the globe back over his head, lowered the lantern, and they moved deeper into the bowels of the hill.

THE light of the lantern fell softly around them, but did not stretch a finger into the darkness ahead. Madman or demon, whatever it was that lay waiting, the killer would stay shrouded in utter darkness until they had come within a few feet. Yet they stood plainly in the light. A sudden leap from the impenetrable blackness, and the thing would strike them down.

But, Marlowe remembered, this flaming pain struck invisibly even in the light. A man, the spiritualist perhaps, had waved his hand in front of Ellen's face and agony had seared her cheek like a white-hot iron. Yet the man had never touched her! And this torture that caused men to twist in agony and die lurked ahead in the darkness, waiting....

The black mouth of the abandoned shaft yawned suddenly to their right, sloping downward. For a moment the two stood hushed in the entrance of the shaft, listening. Silence crowded against them so that their ear drums ached from the very soundlessness. The dank air lay dead and still, as still as the rotting body of a beast buried in an eternity of hideous darkness. Yet Marlowe could feel in the darkness something lurking, waiting....

Marlowe went slowly down the abandoned shaft, with the girl behind him. He could hear, above the muffled sound of his shoes, the heavy hammering of his heart. The vein above his left temple was pounding, and every nerve in him was as taut as a steel spring.

The yellow light rocked slightly as he walked, crawled faintly along the wall to his right. The left wall was hidden in the limitless night.

A black edge showed in the yellow circle. He had reached the end of the shaft. Breath suspended, Marlowe stepped past the shaft's mouth to the edge of the stream, the gun ready in his hand.

Hideous laughter jarred the dead air like the splitting of thousands of tons of rock overhead. The sound bounded along the low ceiling, across the black, still water, to return and crash at Marlowe's ears from every direction.

Wild terror struck at his brain. Madness leaped from the black pit in his belly to clutch bony fingers about his lungs, crushing them.

Marlowe swung up the lantern. The light spun along the rock edge of the stream, struck at the black water, faded.

On the edge of the stream lay the twisted, naked body of Bill Daniels!

In the split second that Marlowe stared, horrified, the man was convulsed in agony, twitched, went still. The swollen, contorted face stared up at Marlowe with a sickening leer.

Ellen Daniels screamed shrilly, rushed past Marlowe as he lay the lantern down near the body of the dead man. "Father!" she cried. "Father!" She snatched the screen from her head, knelt beside him.

Something struck gently at the glass globe about Marlowe's head. He saw a black shadow slip across the globe, sliding around his neck. Marlowe jerked up his hand, struck a wet round thing.

A terrific snatch tore at the glass around his head. It caught under his chin, snapping his head back, jerking him upward, off his feet. He hung swaying in the air.

MADNESS writhed in Marlowe's head, held his brain in an icy clamp. Stark terror surged through him, making him unconscious of the pain that wrenched his neck. Four bloody slits burst into the palm of his left hand where his fingernails bit into the cushioned flesh.

Then, through the glass globe about his head, he saw the disturbed black water of the stream just beyond where Ellen Daniels knelt. A ghastly face and head came out of the water, sent black ripples flowing off into darkness. The face was flat with gigantic, lidless eyes. From its center sprung a strange appendage which might have been a snout, might have been a mouth.

Hanging in the air, Marlowe wrenched himself around, terrific anger thawing the fear that had crushed his lungs. He drew his gun.

Ellen Daniels saw the face and terror choked the scream in her throat. She leaped to her feet, and her body shielded the thing from Marlowe's gun, leaving it barely visible.

The face vanished under the black water. One bare arm lunged upward, clutched the girl's dress, pulled. She staggered forward, hands clutching frantically at the air. A wild shriek rent the darkness.

Then she plunged into the water, pulled by that bare, bodiless arm, her cry cut suddenly short. Black water leaped into the air, swirled back into the trough her body had made. Dark ripples rolled in widening circles, vanished.

Ken Marlowe struggled furiously, feet kicking the air, body swinging helplessly.

A choked cry broke from Marlowe's lips, beat in dulled echoes against the jar about his head. His finger tightened on his gun trigger. The light had glinted on a figure, naked except for a loincloth. And the face was a horrid, flat face with great round lidless eyes. In its hands the thing held a taut rope which stretched upward into darkness.

As Marlowe flung up his gun the figure leaped to one side, let go the rope. Marlowe crashed down, the roar of his gun thundering under the low ceiling.

His feet hit the rock, slipped. He went flat, his head cracking against the rock, shattering the globe. Fighting the numbing horror that clutched his heart and lungs Marlowe leaped to his feet, swung up the lantern. A dense wall of smoke swirled before him, twisting slowly upward.

With a mad cry, Marlowe plunged into the smoke. He whirled the lantern about him in a vicious circle and struck nothing. Breath ripped from his nostrils as Marlowe leaped to the wall, began to make his swift way around it, the lantern held stiffly away from him into the smoke.

Abruptly he stopped. Black water lay at his feet.

He whirled, plunged back through the smoke, swinging the lantern. He burst into the free air.

The swinging light showed the naked, swollen body of Bill Daniels, then black water, black walls, and writhing smoke. Nothing else.

MARLOWE set the lantern at his feet, put his left hand to his neck. He caught the rope noose, jerked it larger, pulled it over his head, cursing hoarsely. Picking up the lantern he held it above him. In the top of the cave a pulley had been fastened, and over it the rope ran.

His foot crunched on a piece of the shattered globe and Marlowe laughed hoarsely, wildly. "So that's how poor Ed Reilly was choked!" he said through lips that seemed stiff and thick. "Thank God, the noose caught around the rim of the globe instead of my neck!"

For a long moment he stood without moving, his left hand holding the lantern stiffly in front of him, the fingers of his right hand like iron strips around the butt of the automatic. His brain battled with horror, his heart pounded cold blood through his body.

Hurriedly, with cold trembling fingers, he sat the lantern on the floor, stuck his gun in his coat pocket, peeled off his coat. Whatever this nameless beast was that had seized Ellen Daniels, it had dragged her under the water. There was no place the other one could have gone except into that dark, oily stream whose waters seemed to stand dead still under the black ceiling of this subterranean sepulcher.

And wherever that hideous, flat-faced creature had taken Ellen Daniels—Ken Marlowe was going after her!

He pulled off his shoes. For a moment he stood, toes hooked over the rock edge of the stream while fear surged through his body. What lay under that black, impenetrable-looking water where the monster had pulled Ellen? What chance did he stand in a fight under water with such a creature? His heart rock-like in his throat, he plunged directly toward the point where the creek seemed to disappear under low shelving rock.

Marlowe gasped as he hit the ice-cold water. Flat on the surface, three feet from where the stream ended, he sucked the dank air deep into his lungs. Then he dove.

He touched slick rock, went deeper, sliding his hands along the wall. He blinked his eyes, but except for the feel of the water he could not tell when they were open. Marlowe's fingers found an opening in the wall and swimming slowly, he moved into it. It was narrow, tunnel-like, and, pulling his arms back in a breast stroke, he felt the slick rock on each side. He let his body rise, struck the wall above. The water filled the tunnel completely.

He dove, touched rock under him. And a new menace showed itself. The water-filled passage was too small to let him turn around.

Marlowe let the air slide from his nostrils, heard the bubbles roll east his ear. His lungs were beginning to ache. Terror gripped him, squeezing breath from him. In a half minute more he'd be gasping water into his lungs. What if this passage had no end?

Then his outstretched fingers touched human flesh. Wild fear surged through him. His fingers gripping frantically on the bare arm he had caught. Marlowe heaved forward. But the body did not move! Groping forward, Marlowe felt wet cloth and under it cold flesh. Then beyond the body he touched solid rock. The waterfilled passage ended abruptly right here!

CATCHING the wrist of the drowned man with his left hand, Marlowe shoved viciously, slid back through the water pulling the body with him.

Swiftly he beat his way backward, towing the body. By putting his free hand against the wall, he got purchase for a crab-like retreat. He clutched the wall again with his right hand, tried to shove off it. The wall was slick and his fingers slid futilely. He held his legs stiff, cupped his right hand back of his wrist, pulled it furiously down and forward.

His lungs ached and he felt sick inside. He had to fight to keep from gulping in mouthfuls of water as he slid backward. Pain tore at his lungs as, almost unconsciously, he towed the body with him.

His back scraped along the ceiling of the tunnel. His legs touched a sharp edge. He threw his hand backward, caught the edge, heaved. Then he was struggling upward. His head burst into dank air.

For twenty seconds Marlowe treaded water. Air rushed into his lungs, strained them until they pressed against his ribs. The air tore through his gaping mouth and he sucked more into his lungs.

He swam slowly to the ledge by the lantern, towing the body. Near the edge of the stream Marlowe released the dead man, let himself down feet first under the water. He touched rock, fought his way along it a step or two, shoved up into the air again.

Catching the ledge with his hands, he whipped the water with his feet, pulled downward with his arms, flipped himself up to the bank. Kneeling, he moved the lantern nearer to the edge where the glow fell on the black water. The body of a man, wearing athletic underwear, floated face down. Marlowe caught an arm and leg, pulled the drowned man to the bank, rolled him over on his back.

The lamp light fell soft and yellow on the pale face of Wilson, the mine foreman. A stain, darker than the water, showed on his chest.

Standing gazing down at the corpse. Marlowe suddenly remembered the stain of blood on the floor at Larvki's.

So this was the man who had dumped the body down the chimney; the man whom his confederates accidentally had killed while firing at Marlowe in that mad fight at the spiritualist's!

CHAPTER SIX

ONE MASK GONE!

HE BENT, picked up his coat, slid into it, then reached for the lantern and stood staring at the water. Diving back now wouldn't help. If Ellen had been held under water all this time she had drowned. There was a chance that somewhere along this ledge the ceiling would be higher with air pockets above the water. Certainly there had to be an outlet somewhere, and Ellen Daniels might be alive in some cavern along the bank of the stream.

He remembered the small flashlight he kept in the pocket of his automobile and the dagger-like letter opener that lay on his desk. The rays of the light wouldn't reach far under water, but they would help—and if he had under-water fighting to do, the knife would be a deadly weapon.

Abruptly he wheeled, began to run up the abandoned shaft. The yellow light of the lantern danced fantastically along the black walls. His foot struck a shallow hole, pitched him forward. Marlowe twisted, swinging the lantern away from the wall. His shoulder struck heavily and he slid to his knees, pain throbbing through his left shoulder, but the lantern was still burning. If that went out and he had to feel his way through the tunnel, it would take him nearly an hour to find the opening. Marlowe staggered to his feet, began to run again.

Halfway up the main tunnel he slowed to a walk. It wouldn't do to be too tired when he got back down to the mouth of the abandoned shaft. Under that black water he'd find somewhere the—the monsters—that had taken Ellen Daniels. And when he did—Marlowe's teeth ground together.

The mouth of the tunnel loomed a gray blur, turning sharp white and black as he moved toward it. The sunlight hurt his eyes even before he had stepped into it, and as he passed from the tunnel he clapped his right hand to his mouth, muffling a sneeze. The sun felt warm and soft through his wet clothes and he felt it beat through his wet hair onto his skull. He went across the small yard to the door of the office, moving with soft, almost noiseless strides.

He pushed open the door, stepped into the office. On the far side of the room where the little safe squatted in a corner, a man leaped to his feet, spun around to face Marlowe. He clutched papers in both hands, and as he spun his big-knuckled fingers crushed them with a nervous, vicious movement. His hard gray eyes glinted savagely.

"WELL," Marlowe said, his voice flat, "so *you're* doing a little private investigating, eh, Brady!"

Brady stood without moving. But into his eyes had crept a look of scorn, of relief.

Swiftly, Marlowe looked around the room. The top of both his and Crim's desks were littered with papers and the drawers stood open. He moved his eyes back to Brady's square, heavy-featured face. "I should warn you," he said quietly, "that investigating around here is a bit dangerous. I was looking at an investigator a few minutes ago. He was—dead!"

A strange flame flashed for a brief instant into Brady's granite eyes, and was gone. When he spoke his words were as crisp, as decisive as ever. "There's no need for me to say what I've been doing. But there is one thing I can say, Mr. Marlowe: You're a damned fool! Mentally, you're a child, and"—Brady surged his heavy shoulders forward—"you're about to get hurt. I'll offer you as much for your half of the mine as yesterday I offered for both halves. Since then things have developed that make it necessary for me to buy you out—and I'm going to get it."

Brady's eyes glinted savagely. "I advise you to take it, Mr. Marlowe." His words went slow, hard, like the sound of heavy rocks falling. "Take it and get out, Mr. Marlowe. Otherwise…." The flame leaped behind his granite eyes again, faded.

"Thanks," Ken Marlowe said softly, "but I sort of like this mine. Sort of a hobby with me; one that I like." He stepped across the office toward Brady and stopped a yard away.

"I'm mighty busy right now," Marlowe said matter-of-factly. "When I've finished the work I've got to do, I'll talk the matter over with you. And"—his shoulders hunched slightly forward and his fingers went stiff and talon-like—"I want to be so certain that you stay and talk with me about it, Mr. Brady, that I'm going to tie you up here so you won't leave while I'm gone. And I'll leave a little note for Frank so that if he comes in he'll know why you are tied and won't untie you."

Again the red flame danced behind Brady's eyes, a flame that glowed and went out, and Marlowe thought he saw a shadow of fear flicker across the man's face. The thick lips twitched, then curled disdainfully.

Brady's hand moved slowly toward his coat pocket. "Don't move for the gun," Marlowe said quietly. "There's been enough killing around here without my doing any of it."

The two men stood unmoving, glaring into each other's eyes. Marlowe was the taller by several inches, Brady wider in the shoulders and hips. Through the window to the right the sunlight streamed in a golden shaft, and through the bar tiny motes swayed endlessly. The curtains that Edith Waters, Crim's fiancée had hung over the office windows, lay as though pressed against the sill, unmoving. The sunlight glinted on the edges, leaving the rest in shadow.

"WELL," Marlowe said calmly, "you can sit in that chair and get tied without being hurt, or…."

Brady stepped backward and his hand flashed toward his pocket.

Marlowe moved like a flash. His right hand smashed upward to Brady's jaw as he lunged forward; his left snaked Brady's wrist. Brady hunched his shoulder and Marlowe's hand drove into his cheek, too high for a knockout. Then Marlowe, holding to Brady's wrist, twisted sharply, heaved. The heavy man was jerked into the air across Marlowe's back and crashed to the floor with the mine operator on top.

For so heavy a man Earle Brady was remarkably fast. He hit the floor rolling, wrenched his hand free, bounded to his feet, gun leaping from his pocket. The blue muzzle flecked up toward Ken Marlowe.

Two feet away was Marlowe's desk. From hands and knees he dived, hit behind it, crouching.

There was a sudden breaking of glass, pieces clattering to the floor. Something hard smashed into the wall above Marlowe to fall with a thud.

In the split second after he hit behind the desk Marlowe heard the glass break, heard the crash against the wall above him. He clapped his open hands against the desk, face almost touching it and drove forward like a football tackle.

The desk smashed into Earle Brady, hurled him backward. The gun roared in the little room, thundered against the walls. Like a cat Marlowe arched his body over the desk, struck Brady who was reeling backward and smashed him to the floor. Marlowe's fingers snapped around the barrel of the gun, pushed it upward.

Brady's fist struck Marlowe's ribs, jarring the air from his lungs. Still twisting on the gun, Marlowe wriggled upward, and drew back his fist to strike again. Toes digging into the floor, Marlowe struck.

The jar ran through his arm to his shoulder, and Brady's head snapped back like the cracker of a whip, bounced against the floor. His eyelids fluttered and the automatic skidded from his hand. Marlowe's right arm went back again. The wrist slightly arched he drove the fist to Brady's chin once more.

Brady's head popped deep to the right and lolled back, listlessly. Marlowe got to his knees, pushing against Brady's chest with his right hand. Then he stood up.

A gaping hole had been smashed in the window panes. The day was hot and the lower sash had been raised. Now both panes were shattered. Sunlight sparkled on the broken glass on the floor.

Marlowe walked around his desk to the far wall. On the floor lay crumpled paper. He picked it up. It was wrapped around a rock the size of an egg. Sticking Brady's gun in his other pocket, he unwrapped the paper. Then he stood staring, puzzled, at it. The paper was perfectly blank!

Holding the paper in his left hand Marlowe stared perplexed at the blank sheet, then quickly stepped to the window and looked out. The ragged hillside, cluttered with rock and low scrub bushes, lay empty under the warm sunshine. To his right he could see the tram line leading down hill; to his left the rugged hill sloped upward.

Marlowe grunted, placed the paper on the warm, sun-brightened window sill, and bent down. Brady was still out, lying flat on his back, hands sprawled over his head. Marlowe caught him under the arms, dragged him into a chair.

He tore the curtains from the window, bound Brady's hands behind the chair, his feet to the chair legs. Then he picked the rock from the floor, slipped it into Brady's mouth, slipped a bit of the curtain over his face and tied it back of his head.

THE man was coming to, his eyes blinking dazedly. "I don't know exactly who you'd call," Marlowe said, "but I don't think you'll call anyone with that gag."

From his desk he picked the paper cutter. When the mine had employed convict labor before the state governor put those men on the roads, a prisoner had made this knife by months of filing on a pick head. A guard had taken it from him and had given it to Marlowe. It had a heavy wooden handle and a blade an inch and a half wide at the base sloping to a needle-like point, sharp on both edges.

Marlowe flipped back his coat, stuck the knife under his belt, started for the door. Abruptly he halted, turned back to the paper lying in the sunshine on the window sill.

Marlowe's mouth and eyes jerked open as he stared, unbelieving at the paper. Crude writing sprawled across the paper that had been blank three minutes before! He read:

This is the last warning! Take what you can get for this mine and get out. For you and your partner there waits only death and torture under this hillside.

There was no signature.

Behind him Marlowe heard a thumping, turned to see Brady wriggling in his chair, his eyes blazing. The corners of Ken Marlowe's mouth went up but there was no humor in the smile. "The note came at the wrong time, huh Brady?" he said softly. "If you had fired a few seconds earlier, perhaps there would have been no need of throwing it. You didn't want to risk anyone but me reading it, so your pal used invisible ink!"

Brady's cheeks puffed but no sound came from behind his gag. He leaned forward, and the legs of the chair scraped along the floor as he twisted. Then his muscles relaxed and he sat staring downward. Marlowe gazed at him for a moment, wheeled and went out the door.

He swung toward the little lot where he had left his car. No road except the tram line ran to the mine itself. He went rapidly, cursing as he walked.

Marlowe rounded a turn in the tram tracks, came on the little parking lot. His car sat where he had left it. Beyond was a taxi, the driver waiting. Crim's car was not there. He'd evidently gone to the city.

Marlowe stepped to his own car, pulled the door open, fished the light from the pocket. Beyond, he saw the taxi driver crawl from his own machine, stand with one foot on the running board looking toward Marlowe He was a small, squat, brown-skinned man with bushy, overhanging brows.

Marlowe stuck the flashlight in the pocket with Brady's gun and said to the driver, "You might as well go on back to town. I'm afraid Mr. Brady will be busy for some time."

The driver's black brows jerked into a straight line. "Dat so!" he snapped, a foreign twang to his voice. "Well, I think I'll stick around. He ain't paid me yit."

"Okay," Marlowe said quietly, "stick around."

He turned and headed up the hill toward the mine. Elder bushes grew alongside the path and blackberry vines wound around them. He stopped, pulled the knife from under his belt, cut a three foot length from one of the elder bushes. As he went up the hill he began cleaning the pith from the hollow stem.

For a moment he stopped at the door of the office, looked in at Brady sitting stiffly in his chair, his cheeks puffed by the rock in his mouth. Marlowe crumpled the white pith of the elder in his hand, tossed it on the floor. "We'll see," he said softly to Brady, who sat cursing him with his eyes, "if the note was correct."

He went on, toward the gaping hole in the hillside.

CHAPTER SEVEN

CRAWLING TORTURE!

*T**WICE BEFORE,*** Marlowe had come down this passage of death, and twice he had been attacked. This time he came wanting a fight. And this time, by God he would not go out until he had found Ellen Daniels and the monsters that had captured her!

The finger of light danced along the tracks ahead of him, and once more he became conscious of the stillness of the place, a stillness so deep that the soft hissing noise of his shoes in the blanket of coal dust seemed to echo against the close-pressing walls.

Pulling his automatic from his pocket, he stepped on, swinging ahead toward the abandoned shaft, toward the spot where death and torture lurked. His breath hissed in his nostrils as he stopped a yard inside the shaft mouth. His gun held close to the flash, showed a dull blur. He could see his knuckles, white from pressure against the gun butt. Then he flung his body past the end of the tunnel in a giant leap. Twisting in the air he whipped his light sharply to the left, gun ready. The light ran like a luminous snake along the black walls, across the black water, whipped along the narrow ledge. Nothing there.

The light snapped around, shot along the rocky ledge, across the bodies of the two dead men, to where the smoke hung like a dark pall. The smoke was deathly still; the light slid into it and faded. One end sprawled along the floor, the other reaching up into darkness, the rope lay as Marlowe had left it.

Shoulders forward, gun ready, Marlowe moved toward the

smoke. It had thinned slightly, but in the dead air of the place it still hung thick, unmoving, blotting up the pencil of light from the flash.

Then Marlowe stepped into the smoke.

It was acrid, burning his eyes, and he felt tears forming in them as he moved, snapping the light from side to side. He reached the far wall, moved along it to the water's edge, then back through the smoke again, into the open air.

From his eyes he wiped the tears the smoke had formed, shot the light around the low-ceilinged vault. Except for himself and the two corpses at the creek's edge, the tomb-like cave was deserted.

His teeth clamped together back of thin-pulled lips. Well, wherever those things were, wherever they had taken Ellen Daniels, he'd find them!

He slid his gun into his hip pocket, adjusted the knife at his belt, took Brady's automatic from his coat, slipped it under his shirt and inside his belt. Then he peeled off his coat, shifting the flash from hand to hand as he pulled his arms through the sleeves. He pulled off his shoes, dropped them beside his coat. They made a loud jarring noise in the utter silence of the cavern.

Ken Marlowe sat down on the edge of the stream, holding the flash in his left hand. With his right hand he pulled the length of elder bush from his coat pocket, then quietly let himself into the water, gasping at its coldness.

When the water reached his chin Marlowe shoved silently away from the bank, treading water. He put one end of the hollow stem in his mouth, let himself down. The water closed blackly over his head.

The rays of the flashlight jabbed into the water, but the heavy blackness seemed to beat them back, crumpling the finger of light into a dull, short blur. It was difficult walking on the bottom. The water held his legs, and with his head tilted to hold one end of the tube in his mouth and the other above the water so that he could breath through it, he could scarcely see the short light flung by the flash.

Slowly, quietly, Marlowe made his way to the bank, began to

feel along it. Where the water had washed pockets in the rock Marlowe jabbed in the light, eyes aching into the darkness around it. With his leg he felt the low, tunnel-like pocket where he had nearly drowned a half hour before.

The water touched him like liquid darkness, and somewhere under here moved the ghastly things that had seized Ellen Daniels, the things that had tortured and murdered her father and two men. He wondered suddenly if the flaming torture that had struck his face, that had caused the two dead miners to writhe and twist before life passed from them could strike under water.

THEN he saw, dully, an opening in the solid rock wall of the stream. It seemed to extend from the bottom to within a foot of the water's surface, and was some four feet wide. Marlowe thrust the light into it—and discovered only darkness. He felt a slow tug of the water, a current.

He slid his hand along the top of the ledge. About two feet inside the opening shot upward, how high he could not tell. Marlowe pressed his toes on the bottom, shot his head out of the water. He pressed the tube against the palm of his left hand, held his right thumb over the other end. Then he dropped until his feet touched the bottom and shoved.

The water had cut an almost perfectly round passage through the earth and rock. In the center the ceiling was not more than a foot and a half above the water which lapped blackly along, the sides. The stream ran straight for some fifty feet, beyond that the light of the flash faded.

Flipping off the light, Marlowe began to swim. Inside him a fierce anger that was almost joy warmed his blood. This stream, he felt sure, led to the place Ellen Daniels had been taken—and led to the fiends that had taken her. He was approaching the end of his search. And, he thought grimly, perhaps the end of his life!

He rounded a corner and stopped, treading water. Ahead of him the creek ended abruptly in a solid stone wall with the ceiling of the tunnel slanting down to join it.

Lying flat on the surface, he jerked his hips into the air, pulled in a vicious breast stroke with his arms, plunged. The dull blur of the flash touched on slick rock. Then he felt the tug of the water again. The rock ledge opened into a narrow hole. He swam into it, pulling his way forward.

As he swung back his arms for the third stroke Marlowe realized that his hands were not touching the sides. He blinked his eyes to make sure they were open. The blackness of the water seemed to fade, growing slowly gray. He let himself start floating toward the top, tugged the automatic from under his belt as he gulped air into his lungs.

A wild cry jarred in his ears, made him spin in the water, bringing his gun up. Then he stopped, and the curse froze on his lips. He remained staring for a long moment, his eyes blinking in the gray light that filtered from an overhead opening.

Ahead the stream lapped along a rocky ledge beyond which stretched a strip of sandy beach, and beyond that a dark, shallow cave. In the distance he heard the muffled rippling of Cataba Creek. This evidently, was where the underground stream met the large creek which half circled the base of the hill.

Marlowe saw these things in the split second that his eyes were leaning toward the point from which the scream had come. Then he stiffened.

On the sandy bar beside the stream were two men—and Ellen Daniels. The girl's wet dress clung closely to the soft curves of her body. One of the men stood behind her, his left arm circling her waist, his right hand holding an automatic, the dark muzzle centered between Ken Marlowe's startled eyes. Both men were naked except for short trunks. And over their, faces they wore gas masks.

These were the hideous figures he had seen at the mouth of the abandoned shaft, and this explained how they remained so long under water.

The short, powerful man behind Ellen had pulled the gas masks slightly loose at his chin so that he could talk but the words were thick and muffled.

"Drop that gun, Ken Marlowe, and come on out. This is the last act."

MARLOWE stared at the man without answering. There was no chance to shoot. He might get the tall, dark-skinned man to the left, but the other was shielded by Ellen, and it was signing his own death warrant to fire. Marlowe dropped the gun. Treading water he wiped the back of his hand across his eyes.

Ellen Daniels' face was drawn and frightened, and her full mouth trembled when she spoke. "Why did you come here, Ken? They'll—they'll kill you!"

The man squeezed her waist roughly. "Shut up!" he snapped. Then to Marlowe, "All right. Are you coming out now, or are you going to wash out—with a bullet through your head?"

Through thin lips Marlowe said softly, "I'm coming out." He swam to the bank, slid himself on it, stood up. "All right," he asked, "now what?"

The man back of Ellen Daniels spoke out of the corner of his month, his voice barely intelligible back of the mask. "Get that knife out of his belt and see if he's got anything else."

Swiftly the other stepped to Marlowe, pulled the knife from his belt. He grunted softly as he looked at it. For a moment Marlowe stood unmoving, his heart beating high. He glanced upward, at the patch of daylight, twenty feet above. A rough ladder led up to the opening.

Perhaps this fellow would overlook the automatic in his hip pocket—then if the other would step from behind Ellen....

Over the fellow's shoulder, just under the edge of the cave, Marlowe saw a small paper box. With its red commercial lettering on the side it looked oddly out of place. Marlowe smiled grimly. Smoke bombs, of course! That had caused the sudden smoke bursting from the earth, the smoke behind which these men had slipped into the water and vanished!

Carefully, the dark-skinned man patted Marlowe's sides, his flank. With another grunt he pulled the blunt-nosed gun from the mine operator's hip. Turning, he carried the gun into the shallow cave, dropped it on the sand. The other man flung Ellen to one side, said into his mask. "Bring out the deeds we've got ready for this fellow. He'll want to see them."

As the girl was pushed to one side she staggered in the sand, caught herself, stopped. Eyes following her, Ken Marlowe saw for the first time a strange container near the mouth of the cave. It was a dome-shaped jar of fine screening. And the inside was black with swarming, crawling insects. Ants, millions of tiny black ants! At the bottom of the jar was a spigot-like place through which a few could be allowed to come at a time.

In Marlowe's mind flashed a hideous picture of the body of Bill Daniels, black with gnawing, stinging ants, shooting their fiery poison through every agonized nerve. Then, the body washed in the creek, the swollen corpse had been left on the bank.

This, then, was the torture of which the note had warned! The muffled voice of the man jarred on Marlowe's ears, set his nerves quivering like taut bands.

"Now you know why the bodies you found were so twisted with agony, and why they were so puffed and swollen. In South America those are called fire ants, and if a man is stung by one he will put the live end of his cigarette to the place—the pain of the fire is less. Those that stung you and the girl were gentle. Most of their venom had been extracted by stinging—something else—shortly before. If a few thousand of those get on a man they kill him—but not too quickly. In South America men had rather be burned at the stake than—tied on an ant hill!"

He paused, and Marlowe could feel sheer horror creep like a cold snake along his spine as he stared with bulging eyes toward the deathly, venomous insects.

Then the man said, his voice low: "But there is no need for you to know about them—if you are sensible."

Slowly, Marlowe turned his head to face the other. Behind the glass plates he could see hard, gray eyes. "All right," he said softly, "I may have the brain of a child but I already know all I want to about ants." He paused, added, "What is it you want?"

From the tall, dark-skinned man who still held Marlowe's knife between long brown fingers, the gray-eyed killer took a sheaf of papers, held them out to Marlowe. "Write your name on those," he said, "and you'll be free—to live."

Rapidly, Marlowe looked at them. It was a bill of sale for his half of the mine. The purchaser was unnamed. As he read, Marlowe's body seemed to drain itself of emotion and a cold, dead feeling crept through his belly toward his heart. It was not fear—it was too late for fear. But it was the sick, empty feeling that comes to a brave man faced by certain death.

For Ken Marlowe knew he would not be released after he had signed over the mine. Released, he had only to locate the owner to find the fiendish murderer of the miners and of Bill Daniels. Marlowe raised his eyes to the hard ones behind the flat glass. There was only certain death in their gray-blue flame.

"Yes," Ken Marlowe said, "sign—but I'll be free—to die!"

A snarl came from under the mask. "You had your chance to sell. I warned you!"

Through thin, unmoving lips Marlowe pushed the words, "If you had thought there was any chance I'd do it, you'd never had that rock thrown. You knew I wouldn't back out—after you had the girl."

The man laughed shortly, harshly. "Hell, we've done enough talking. Are you going to make out this bill now, or"—his voice dropped, each word falling on Marlowe's consciousness like the slow dripping of water—"are you going to let those ants eat on you until you are willing—or until you look like those bodies you found?"

Marlowe's eyes jerked instinctively toward the screen container where millions of horrid fire ants crawled in layers. Shrinking away from the glass, Ellen Daniels watched him with large, dark eyes. Her Titian hair, dark with water, hung about her shoulders, and one bar of sunlight, reaching down through the opening twenty feet overhead, shot tiny spangles of flame through the wet curls.

Then Ken Marlowe looked back into the eyes behind the glass plates of the mask. "A half hour," he said slowly, "after she goes up that ladder and out of sight, I'll sign."

"No! No! They'll kill you!"

The girl swept to him, catching his shirt in her hands, her slender fingers working nervously in the wet linen. "They'll kill you!" she repeated.

Ken Marlowe looked into her eyes and shook his head slowly.

He slid his hands along her forearms, took her fingers from his shirt. "They are going to kill me anyway," he said gently. "They can't afford to let me go. But I'll see that you get out of here—safely."

The girl swayed close to him and her hands slipped toward his shoulders. "I don't want to go," she whispered, "without you."

The man holding the automatic laughed and Marlowe spun to face him, his body stiffening. "Don't worry," the man sneered. "You won't get out of here—without him. Or with him." The flat glass eye-pieces jerked toward Marlowe. "I can't let her go anymore than I can let you go. For the same reason."

CHAPTER EIGHT

OUT OF THE PIT

MARLOWE DID not answer, and the words of the killer purred hollowly back into the shallow cave, faded like gray smoke. The girl's body swayed closer to Marlowe and he could hear her forced breathing.

Marlowe felt his heart beating under his ribs with a faint, far-away hammering while the hair along his nape rose stiffly. He had faced death for himself with only a cold hatred for the murderer, but now—death for Ellen....

His lips snarling, Marlowe said, "Until you let her go I don't sign—not for all the ants in hell!"

The man moved the black muzzle of the gun in a slow circle centering about Marlowe's belly. "Perhaps. If they were all on you. You're a brave fool, Ken Marlowe. But if half the ants," he moved lust-glinted eyes toward the girl, then back, "were crawling about her naked body, then perhaps you would sign."

Air lurched through clinched teeth into Marlowe's lungs. "God!" he gasped. "You—you can't torture her!" Only a fiend, an inhuman monster would release these deadly monsters on this girl to mutilate and deform her; to make that slim, lovely body a grotesque and evil mass of lumpy, bloated flesh. For himself he was not afraid. He could stand any torture they might inflict—any except hearing the agonized screams of this girl. "You can't torture *her*," he repeated frantically.

"And I can't let her go either," the man sneered. Out of the corner of his mouth he spat the words toward his companion, "Strip her!"

Ken Marlowe caught the girl by the waist, pulled her behind him. He half crouched, elbows at his waist, forearms straight in front, fingers claw-like. His face was a flaming mask of hate as he stood, waiting. The tall man snaked forward. He had caught the knife by the grip and his wrist arched slightly as he advanced.

"Stop!" the man with the gun ordered. The tall man halted in his tracks, knife ready. Marlowe half turned to face the man who had spoken. He had lowered the gun, and the black muzzle centered on Marlowe's leg between thigh and knee. "Come around in front of him, sister," he snapped. "And be quick before you have to step over him."

Anger flamed in Marlowe's blood but he fought to keep from plunging toward the gunman. If he dived and was shot, he left Ellen Daniels at the mercy of these two fiends. Dead, or lying helpless on the ground with a bullet through his leg, there was no possible chance of saving her. Alive and uninjured there was always hope.

THE muscles in his arms and shoulders quivered as the girl stepped from behind him, moved slowly toward the man who stood holding the knife. Her face was pale and drawn; her eyes were dark fires and her full lips were compressed and steady. She stopped, and stood, head bowed, looking at the ground.

With his left hand the man caught her dress at the throat, jerked. The girl staggered, nearly losing her balance as the wet cloth ripped loudly. The man bent, caught the dress, ripped again. It fell from her shoulders, but the seam at the bottom held. For a moment the man stood looking at her, his eyes almost invisible back of the glass plates. Then he cut the seam with the knife.

With a jerk he removed the rest of her clothing.

Ken Marlowe could see the little muscles in the girl's shoulders and knees quivering as she stood naked, unmoving, eyes on the ground. Slowly Marlowe twisted his head toward the gunman, body still crouched. The man's lust-brightened eyes flashed back to Marlowe, and the gun was rock-steady at his belly. "Strip yourself. We won't be niggardly with these ants. Give them plenty of room to bite."

Marlowe's fingers fumbled with the buttons of his shirt, but his eyes never left the muzzle of the gun. If for one second it would waver, steel-springed muscles would fling him forward. But the gun did not waver.

Peeling the wet shirt from broad, hard shoulders Marlowe wondered if, after the bullet struck him, he could reach the man with strength enough left in him to twist the gun away. Even if he did, the other would be on him before he could turn, and if he killed one and was killed, Ellen Daniels would be left unprotected, with the tall, dark-skinned man whose eyes were dancing flames behind the glass plates of his mask.

Marlowe slid out of his trousers and trunks, dropped them on the ground near where the girl's torn dress lay. "Tie them," the gunman snapped. His confederate went back into the cave, returned with two lengths of small rope. He stuck the knife under the belt of his trunks, stepped back of Marlowe.

"Cross your hands behind you," the man said. Marlowe did, and felt the bite of the rope as the knot was jerked tight. Without warning Marlowe's legs buckled as his captor kicked the back of his knees. He hit the sand hard.

The fellow tied the rope that bound Marlowe's wrists to a jagged outcropping of rock. Pushing Marlowe flat on his back, he ran the rope up his side, around his neck, back to the rock, and pulled it taut.

Marlowe writhed slowly on the ground, testing the ropes while Ellen Daniels was tied to a rock just beyond. He could reach the rope running up his side by twisting his wrist, but it was too taut to allow him to sit up. His legs, untied, stretched straight on the sand.

"Now," the heavy-built murderer said, "we'll see how you stand up under this."

The killer stepped to the ant-filled cage behind Marlowe's head, turned the spigot at the bottom gently. Then he passed Marlowe, and stopped near his confederate, a couple of yards beyond Marlowe's heels. "I want to watch your face," he smiled pleasantly, "when the ants reach you."

TWISTING his head so that his chin dug into the sand, rolling his eyes into the top of his head until they ached, Marlowe looked back at the screened cage. From it, across the sand, single file, crawled a black line of ants. His eyeballs popped with the strain of looking back, but he could not take them from that terrible black trickle creeping toward him. Marlowe could see the hideous legs of the first fire ant moving stiffly as it approached, reaching straight out from the shiney black body, then bending downward to touch the sand.

He could feel his blood chill in his veins and he writhed fiercely against the rope that held him. The rope scraped flesh from his wrist and warm, sticky blood began to seep along his skin.

Then he saw, as if magnified, the great, ghastly head of the deadly insect less than an inch from his own eyeball.

With a gasp of terror he snapped his head around to save his eye. Wild red flame seemed to burst from his shoulder. The flame seared along his flesh toward his neck as though a white-hot iron had been pushed across the skin. Fighting at the rope that bound him, he tore the flesh around his wrists until the blood ran freely, but he did not feel the pain.

Above him the cold, fiendish voice said, "After they have crossed you they will reach the girl. There will be plenty, more than plenty."

Writhing under the agony, Marlowe fought to keep his voice steady. He couldn't let this inhuman torture happen to her, he *couldn't!* "If you'll kill her quickly, I'll sign. Then you can—can do what you want."

Marlowe felt the sneer in the man's words. "I might make the bargain that way." He spun the gun on his finger.

As the torture seared through his shoulder into his neck Ken Marlowe twisted sharply. His flame-racked brain leaped—there was one chance!

Flattening on his back, Marlowe flung his feet over his head, far back. From the corner of his eye he saw the screen cage with its thousands of ants, the black procession from hell crawling, crawling across the sand toward him. He clamped his feet on both sides of the cage, hurled it toward the men!

As Marlowe had flung his feet behind him the man made a mad clutch at the gun spinning on his finger, fumbled it. Then he lunged desperately as Marlowe hurled the cage. The dark-skinned man tried to leap past him, slipped, shoved. The gunman dropped the automatic, fell sprawling in the sand.

The cage crashed into the chest of the other, and ripped apart! A dark cloud of stinging ants enveloped him, and others fell in great piles to the sand.

With a shriek of agony the man flung his knife away, plunged headlong into the stream to disappear under the rocks that separated the cave from Cataba Creek and the sun outside.

Ken Marlowe's legs moved like a snake striking. He hit the knife with his foot, kicked it against his bound hands, hacked wildly at the rope around his wrists, ripping flesh.

The gunman had staggered to his feet again. He flicked his eyes toward the weapon he had dropped. It was buried in a swarm of ants. Flinging sand with his feet he whirled, leaped for the other gun inside the cave. Ken Marlowe hurled the knife.

The heavy wooden shaft struck the man at the base of the skull, driving him forward. He fell on his face, skidded. Marlowe heard Ellen Daniels gasp as the first ant touched her.

Even as he leaped after the knife Marlowe beat frantically at the half dozen ants on his neck and shoulder, smashing them against his skin. Hot pain flamed through him as he scooped up the knife, leaped back to the girl, slashed her free.

One sharp glance showed hundreds of ants floating on top the water where the man had dived. Marlowe caught up some clothes, grabbed the girl by the hand and leaped for the rough ladder that led to the sunshine above. Hand over hand he raced up after her.

A scream below stopped him and he turned. The murderer had staggered to his feet, caught up the gun from inside the cave and sprung back, brought the muzzle up toward Marlowe. But with his eyes upward he had stepped barefooted into a black cloud of ants!

With a cry of anguish he dropped the gun, dived for the ladder, caught it. Half way up he stopped, beat at the swarming horde of ants with one hand, began to climb again.

Marlowe flipped himself to the top, threw the garments out on the rocks and then stretched out with his hands swinging down along the ladder. As the masked face reached his hands, he caught the mask, tore it off.

And the pain-maddened eyes of Frank Crim stared up at him!

Savagely, Crim snatched for the mask. Marlowe jerked away and Crim clawed again for the mask, clutching with both hands. His fingers caught, slipped. He staggered sharply.

With a frightened shriek Crim lost his balance, plunged backward, his arms beating wildly at the air. He struck, half standing, on the rock ledge of the stream, reeled, for a dizzy second and then plunged backward into the sand.

The bone in Crim's leg snapped as he struck the rock with a sharp cracking noise. Marlowe saw the jagged white bone below the knee rip through the flesh.

Even as Marlowe looked, ants blackened Crim's body; thousands of them swarming hungrily over it. The pain-widened eyes suddenly went black as stinging ants swarmed across the pupils.

Crim's shriek, blood-curdling, terrific, filled the deep hole, echoed wildly in the shallow cave. He clawed at the air, beat the sand. His fingers, striking the sand, dug through the ants that blackened it, showing the white grains. Then, at once, it was black with ants again.

Behind him Marlowe, heard Ellen Daniels' horrified gasp. He stood up, pushed her gently from the mouth of the hole. "Don't look," he said. "It's not pretty. Ahao Larvki can thank his Hawaiian Gods that he got out of there, even though he's only getting into the electric chair. A naked Hawaiian doesn't stand much chance of getting away. The police will have him in a few hours."

When they had hastily struggled into the scanty garments which Marlowe had secured back in the cave, the girl looked up at him from wide, violet-blue eyes. She said, "I don't understand what's happened, what's going to happen. I—"

"It's all over," Marlowe said softly. "Crim had been cheating me for some time about the mines. They were better than I knew, but I trusted him with the books. Lately I had suspected him, but wasn't certain until Brady, after going through the books, offered me twice as much for my half of the mine as he had before.

"After Crim had found the mine to be richer than he had thought at first, he wanted to buy me out, but he didn't want to pay much. He tried to frighten the labor so that no one would work here, then he figured I would sell cheaply. After a year or two people would have forgotten about the terror, and then he could put the mines back in operation.

"He hired the fortune-teller to frighten the men, and when that wasn't a complete success he tried this method."

Ellen's eyes widened. "But if he had bought your half and then put the mines back to work, wouldn't you have known? Why didn't he kill you at first?"

Marlowe nodded and smiled cryptically. "You see, he didn't plan to buy the mine under his own name. He would have sold his half too, buying the whole thing again under an assumed name, through the probate office and the whole transaction carried out by mail. No one here would have ever known who really owned the mine.

"At first he didn't want to kill me because he wanted to buy the mine without going to a public sale to do it.

"Of course, he was willing to kill me today or last night at Larvki's to protect himself. But he tried to keep from killing me at first because he was afraid of the consequence. The police here don't spend much time investigating the death of a worker in a mine. But my family is pretty well known and if I was killed it would stir up an investigation—and Crim didn't want that.

"That's why I thought it was Crim; Brady, being from the North, might not take that angle into consideration. But I was with Frank when the first murder occurred—he had his own men do that—and it threw me off the track. I wasn't certain until a note was flung through the window. But before that I had Brady tied."

"And father," the girl asked, her lips trembling, "what was he doing?"

"Your lather," Marlowe said gently, "was a brave man and very sincere in his efforts to help labor. From the Negro miners he heard rumors of what was happening and began to investigate. He"—Marlowe's shoulders shrugged—"found out too much.

"It's the same thing that happened to Everet Starlin. He liked ghost stories and this interested him so he began to investigate. He had found out too much, even before he went to Larvki's after he had heard that the medium had predicated the deaths. It was his last ghost story. An autopsy'll show just how he was poisoned."

They went down the hillside toward Cataba Creek showing dully through the leaves of the elder and willow bushes on its bank. "If you'll wait here," Marlowe said, "I'll go up to the mine and get us some more clothes—if you are willing to wear dirty overalls. And when I get back—" he paused.

The girl turned dark, wide eyes toward his face and her lips smiled softly. "You started to say something in the mine," she whispered.

Marlowe grinned. "And there, a few minutes ago, you said you did not want to leave without me?"

"Yes."

"Would you be willing," he said slowly, "not to ever leave, any place at all, without me?"

She half closed her eyes while her soft lips waited for him to take his own answer.

THE END

Printed in Great Britain
by Amazon